THE KREW

KRIS KNIGHT

ISBN: 0692438122
ISBN 13: 9780692438121

Chapter 1

It was six o'clock in the morning when Blazz was awakened by the alarm clock going off on the nightstand.

"It's time," he thought to himself, climbing out of his hotel bed where a girl he barely knew still slept.

A smile appeared on his face as he recalled last night's episode. He quickly threw his clothes on, grabbed his gun from under the bed and headed for the mini fridge in the corner of the room. Inside was a half-eaten burrito from Taco Mama, some orange juice and a small bottle of water. He grabbed the bottle of water and closed the door just as his cell phone began to ring.

"Hello?" he answered. "What's up, my nigga?"

The voice replied, "Shit. Ready to get paid. Where the fuck you at?"

"I'm in front, dawg."

"Alright, here I come."

Blazz put his phone away, then walked by the girl still laid out naked on the bed. She turned over on her back, revealing her large, beautiful breasts.

Opening her eyes, she smiled at him. "What time is it?"

"6:15, ma. But check it out. I have to go handle something with my people. Then I'll be right back, ok?"

"Ok, but you better come back, Brian."

Blazz was caught off guard when he heard his name come from her lips. He surely couldn't remember hers at the moment.

"Don't trip. I got you," he said as he ran out the door.

T-Mack was parked in front of the hotel in his Escalade truck on 26" black and chrome rims. As soon as he spotted Blazz, he quickly unlocked the door.

"What up, my nigga?" Mack said with a big grin. "You ready to get your hands dirty?"

Blazz shook his head yes. He was nervous as hell, but he could never let T-Mack know.

They pulled out and drove up Century headed towards the 405 Freeway.

"We got to be in and out fast. Five minutes tops," T-Mack explained while rolling a blunt. "We can't fuck this shit up, so don't half-step this, fool. It has to be taken care of today."

"Yeah, I'm ready. But I don't think we should smoke that shit right now, Mack. If I get high, I ain't gonna to be able to stay focused." Blazz had just gotten out of Juvenile Hall, so he wanted to do everything he could to keep from going back.

"Naw, we gonna light this thing up on the way home," T-Mack replied.

They got on the 10 Freeway headed east and drove for a while until they reached the industrial part of downtown Los Angeles. T-Mack turned off on Alameda and followed the directions Leelee had given them.

"He said turn right on this street coming up and we will see it," Blazz blurted out as he read the directions.

Mack made the turn and both men quickly spotted what they were looking for on the opposite side of the street. Mack then made a U-turn and pulled directly behind an old '88 Honda Accord that had been stolen and left there six hours earlier. Neither of them moved to get out. They had to be sure the coast was clear. The last thing they needed was some nosy neighbor or Good Samaritan calling the cops.

After a few minutes, T-Mack decided it was safe and time to move. "Ok, let's go."

Blazz hopped out first. He put his gloves on, grabbed the screwdriver, and then walked over to the G-ride. He opened the unlocked door and jammed the screwdriver in the already busted ignition. It started the car up immediately. Blazz checked the gas just to be on the safe side, even though they were only going right around the corner. The tank was half full. That was more than enough gas to get them to their destination and back.

Mack opened the passenger door and got in. "Did you leave your phone in the truck? The last thing we need is you fuckin' around and dropping that shit…"

"Come on, man. You know me better than that, Mack," Blazz replied, cutting him off.

They had been over the whole lick from beginning to end several times on the way, and Blazz didn't feel like hearing it again. He was trying to keep his nerves in check, but all the instructions T-Mack kept giving him were not helping. This was the first time that Mack had taken Blazz on a job with him and he wanted to be sure things went as planned. The last thing he wanted was for something to go wrong or for one of them to get caught or hurt.

Mack and Blazz were brothers. They shared the same father, but different mothers. Blazz was seventeen years old and stood 6'2". He weighed 192 pounds with a mocha-brown complexion and light brown eyes. He was definitely considered fine by all the girls at Jefferson High where he played football. He had been the starting wide receiver and star of the team until he got knocked for stealing cars. He had to serve six months in Juvenile Hall and had just been released yesterday.

T-Mack was the oldest at twenty-two. He was tall, but came up an inch shorter than his younger brother. He made up for it in size, however. He weighed 225 pounds and not one ounce of it was fat. He had spent four years locked down in the California Youth Authority for a robbery he had committed with two of his homies from Bloodstone Villain, a street gang from the lower east side of South Central Los Angeles. While he was locked up, T-Mack had taken up boxing. Once he was released, he earned his Golden Gloves.

Blazz pulled away from the curb and drove the short, two-block distance to their destination. Mavericks was a strip club located in a rundown industrial part of Los Angeles, an area mostly deserted on the weekend until the club opened its doors for business at 12 noon. The owner, Nick Wilson, would arrive at 9 am every Sunday to remove and count the money from a large safe located in his private office. When his security arrived an hour later, he would discreetly take the cash out the back door and head for his house. The club money was good, but the real score came from the ecstasy pills that were kept stockpiled in the club. Nick was a member of Wild Style, an outlaw biker gang that manufactured ecstasy and distributed the drug along the entire West Coast.

"There's his car over there," Mack announced. "He should still be by himself. Security will be arriving in about thirty minutes, so let's get this party started. You got the key?"

"Yeah, it's right here," Blazz replied, taking the key from his front pocket and holding it up so Mack could see.

"Let's move then. Remember: just follow my lead and don't do nothing stupid. Ok?"

"Yeah ok, I got it, Mack. Calm down. I ain't about to fuck shit up."

Even though he spoke with confidence, Blazz had never been so nervous. Up until now, he had very little criminal experience, but what he and T-Mack were about to pull off would catapult him into the big league.

"Let's go then."

They pulled their ski masks down over their faces, checked their weapons, and then exited the vehicles. They moved quickly along the side of the building, making sure to stay out of the cameras' range of sight. They made it all the way to the back entrance undetected. Blazz pulled the key out and slowly slid it into the lock. He crossed his fingers, took a deep breath and then turned the key. The lock clicked as he applied pressure to the key.

"Bingo." They were in.

Mack stepped in first with his forty Glock pointed straight ahead. He stopped to listen. Everything seemed cool, so he motioned to Blazz to come in and shut the door. The hallway turned pitch black once the door was closed, and it took a few seconds for their eyes to adjust. Mack looked around and saw that they were by the back dressing rooms in which the strippers changed their outfits.

They slowly crept up the hallway until they came to a door that was slightly cracked open. Mack heard a voice coming from inside and on the door there was a gold-plated plaque that read, "Owner." A red and white sign with the words "STAY OUT" was also taped to the door.

"I'm sorry, babe. I can't do it… If you miss today, I'm going to have to fire you… Look, Rita. If you can get someone else to fill in for you then ok, but this is the last time. I'm trying to run a business here."

Mack could tell by the conversation that the owner was on the phone with one of the dancers. He decided to wait until he hung up before making a move. Blazz was standing directly behind T-Mack ready to spring into action. He was sweating profusely, but his nerves no longer bothered him. The adrenalin running through his veins was giving him courage beyond imagination.

"Well, call me back and let me know." The owner slammed down the phone so hard he nearly broke it.

"Goddamn bitches," he mumbled to himself.

Mack slowly pushed the door open. The owner had his back to him as he shoved money into a bag that sat on his desk. Mack turned to Blazz and gave him the thumbs up sign, letting him know it was showtime.

They bust into the room with their guns drawn.

"Get the fuck on the ground, bitch!" T-Mack shouted.

The owner turned around so fast, he almost fell down. When he saw the two men with ski masks on and the large barrels of their pistols within inches of his face, he nearly pissed on himself.

"WHAT THE FUCK? Ok, ok. Just take the money. Take everything. Just don't kill me, please," he begged.

"Get the fuck down right this fucking minute or I will blow your fuckin' head off, bitch!" Blazz yelled.

He was so pumped up on the high from his newly found power, he almost forgot T-Mack was the one that was in control. The owner dropped down to the floor and lay on his stomach. Fearing for his life made him feel the need to cooperate with their demands.

Mack jumped over him and finished loading the rest of the money in the bag. The safe was still open and he could see another big black duffle bag sitting at the bottom. He slid across the top of the desk, then knelt down and took a look inside. The duffle bag was filled with ziplocs of ecstasy, each bag containing different colored or stamped pills inside. T-Mack closed the duffle bag back up and slung it over his shoulder.

"You got the money, so just take it and leave!" The owner had a bad feeling they had come for something more.

Mack walked over to Blazz and handed him the sack with the money.

"I got it from here, bro," he said, relieving Blazz from his duty of watching over the owner.

Blazz knew what was coming. He grabbed the bag and took a few steps back, but remained in the room to bear witness to the act.

"Please just leave. You got what you came for. There's no reason to kill me....Please. Oh god, help me. Don't kill me," the owner begged with tears running down his face and snot running down his nose.

He reminded T-Mack of his time spent in youth prison, a facility also known as the California Youth Authority. It was filled with young boys crying and begging to god, asking him to protect their lives and their manhood, but all the crying and praying never stopped the devil from showing up at their doors to do his job.

T-Mack aimed the semi-automatic pistol at the back of Nick Wilson's head and pulled the trigger three times.

BAM BAM BAM.

And just like that, the owner's time here on Earth was over.

T-Mack put his gun away and took off running, headed for the back door. Blazz had never seen a person executed before. He was shook up by the whole experience, but snapped back to reality when he felt his brother almost knock him down as he ran past. He took one more look at the corpse before he turned and followed T-Mack.

Ten minutes later they were back on the freeway headed for T-Mack's house. "All clear, little bro. We home free baby. We on the freeway now."

Blazz got up from the floor of the truck and climbed into the front with T-Mack.

"Why the fuck you make me ride back there?" he complained.

"You got to throw the cops off, you know? They don't really fuck with a nigga rolling solo," T-Mack explained.

"Man, Mack, that shit was crazy. But we did that shit. We really pulled it off!"

Blazz was excited; he had never taken part in anything so mind-blowing. "It was like the rush of stealing a car multiplied by ten."

"From here on out we a team. You my right hand man. I'm teaching you everything I know about the game."

Mack never wanted this life for Blazz, but now that he was in, Mack was happy he had someone in the crew that he could really trust.

"Now fire that shit up, blood. It will ease your mind."

Blazz grabbed the blunt and pushed in the truck's cigarette lighter. He hit play on T-Mack's stereo and Lil WEEZY bumped hard as he turned the volume up loud, pushing the three 15" subwoofers to their limit.

I think I love her like pussy, money, weed...

Blazz hit the blunt three times and passed it to his brother, then lay back in his seat. He gazed out the window. The sun was shining and the sky was clear. He had just been released from the halls the other day and had already taken part in a murder-robbery that made him more money than he had ever had in his young life.

Chapter 2

Twenty minutes later across town, Kat paced back and forth in the living room of her and Mack's Westchester condo holding her cell phone. She was beginning to panic. She had been calling T-Mack's phone for the last 15 minutes to make sure everything had gone ok.

"They should have been back by now," she mumbled to herself.

She hated when he didn't answer his phone. If something were to happen to him, she would be devastated. T-Mack meant everything to her. He was the first man to make her feel complete. She had no worries since he had come into her life. She knew with him she would always be safe. Up until she meet Mack, her experience with men was anything but good.

The Past:

"You got the money? Let me see how much it is!" The smoked out forty-year-old black man held his dirt-covered hand out, waiting for the trick to reveal what he had to offer.

"It better be enough for both of us, nigga!" a woman yelled.

She was sitting half-naked on the bed, waiting in anticipation of the quick high she was about to receive once they called the connect.

"FUCK THAT SHIT, MAN! THAT AIN'T ENOUGH!" the black man yelled as he eyeballed the twenty-dollar bill the trick shoved into his hand.

Kathrin sat silently on the floor of the rundown hotel building that she called home. She listened carefully to the grownup's negotiating while she bounced an old yellow ball on the worn out floor. Kathrin knew exactly what they were arguing about. The same scene had been playing out day in and day out for the last year ever since she turned six, so she knew what was coming next. Tears silently rolled down her cheeks. She was careful not to cry out loud from fear of the beating she would receive.

"Girl, stop bouncing that ball and get your ass over here," the Asian woman called out to her daughter.

Kathrin quickly wiped her tears away with the back of her petite hand, then jumped up and ran to her mother's side. She pulled on the long, white tee shirt her mother wore to gain access to the top of the mattress, and then sat still with her head and eyes facing the floor. She always tried to avoid seeing their faces. She didn't want to relive the horrible event over and over again in her dreams, so instead she would try to think of good things that she liked, like ice cream and cake and cartoons. Sometimes when she tried hard enough, she wouldn't even feel them inside her. She would be so far away sometimes, her father would have to slap her in the face to bring her back to reality.

"Yeah, that's what I'm talking about, nigga!" Kathrin's father was finally satisfied once the trick gave up another twenty dollar bill.

He couldn't wait to run across the hall so he could spend it all at the dope spot. He would have settled for far less, but he always played the hold out game with the tricks, making sure to get every cent they were willing to spend.

When he first meet Kathrin's mother she was a fifteen-year-old runaway. He took her in, and then turned her out, getting top dollar for her young, beautiful Filipino body -- even while she was pregnant with Kathrin. He sold her like wine out of a downtown LA liquor store. Then once the streets stole her mother's beauty, the tricks started to turn their gazes towards a very young version of her. Kathrin's father didn't think twice about selling his daughter's soul to the highest bidder, because he had already taken her purity years ago.

"That's for sex with the girl and the mother, right?" the white man asked, making sure everything was clear.

"Yeah, nigga. That's what I fucking said, didn't I? But check it out. Don't go beating on the girl or nothing cruel like that, cause I don't need social services in my business," he ordered, reaching for the door.

A big smile spread across his ashy face at the thought of all the dope he was about to smoke.

"Freeze, you son of a bitch!" was the greeting he received once he opened the door up.

Police officers filled the small hallway, rushing into the room with guns and badges. He tried to run for the window in hopes of escape, but once he turned around, the trick hit him dead in the face, breaking his nose and knocking him out cold.

"LAPD!" the trick yelled as he pointed his pistol and waved his badge at the unconscious dope fiend.

The officers filed into the room, making sure it was secure. Kathrin sat on the bed crying silently as she watched the officers take her parents away in handcuffs. A woman officer came up to her, and then got down on one knee so she would be eye level with her.

"What's your name, sweetie?" she asked with a big smile.

She pulled a small brown teddy bear from behind her back and held it out to the child.

"My name is Kathrin." Her voice was barely more than a whisper and she kept her eyes aimed at the floor.

"Kathrin. That's a beautiful name, sweetie. Kathrin, can I pick you up so we can get you out of here and get you something to eat and a nice hot bath? We can even stop by McDonald's if you like."

At the mention of her favorite restaurant, the girl perked up just a little and slowly shook her head yes.

"Ok sweetie," the officer said as she gently picked Kathrin up off the bed and held her to her chest.

Kathrin wrapped her little legs around the woman's waist and her arms were wrapped tightly around her neck. She peered over the woman's shoulder, taking one last look at the cheap hotel room that she once called home.

"No daddy… Please don't make me do it again…I promise to be good. I promise, I promise! Please mommy, help me! Help me, mommy!" Kathrin suddenly woke up from her nightmare.

She sat up and wiped the sweat from her face, looking around. At first she couldn't remember where she was. As she glanced around a dimly lit room, she noticed that the walls had princesses and fairies painted on them, and it all came back to her. She was at her foster home. Soon she would be adopted and taken to an even better place. At least that's what Ms. Walker had told her. But Kathrin couldn't imagine a place better than Ms. Walker's house. At Ms. Walker's, there was always something fun for her to do. There was a swing set in the back yard, along with a slide and a merry-go-round. The kitchen was full of food and Kathrin never got in trouble for asking for something to eat or drink. She always had lots of clothes and Ms. Walker let her take a warm bath every night. She would brush her hair and put it in two long ponytails with barrettes, just how Kathrin had seen other little girls' hair whenever her mother would take her out of the house. The thing Kathrin loved the most was that there were no men around to bother her and force her to do things her young mind could not comprehend. She lay back down and drifted back to sleep.

It felt like she had just closed her eyes when Ms. Walker came knocking on her door to wake her up for breakfast, but in truth it had been hours.

"Kandy Kat, it's time to wake up!" Ms. Walker came into the room and sat down on the bed, gently nudging her.

Kathrin opened her eyes, then smiled at the woman who had been taking care of her the last seven months.

"Good morning, Ms. Walker!" her gentle little voice called out.

"It is a good day, babe. Some nice people coming to see you today, so you brush your teeth and wash your face and come eat breakfast. Then I'll comb your hair and help you get dressed, ok?"

"Who's coming to see me? Is it Ms. Taylor? I like her!" Kathrin announced, referring to the psychiatrist that had been working with her ever since she arrived at the foster home.

"No baby. It's not Ms. Taylor. It's a surprise, ok? So stop asking questions and run along and clean yourself up so you can eat," Ms. Walker explained with a big smile on her face.

She watched Kathrin as she got up and skipped to the bathroom in her Dora the Explorer nightgown. Ms. Walker thought back to the terrible conditions Kathrin was in when she first arrived at Rainbow Castle, the foster home she ran. Kathrin would barely speak. She was afraid of everything that came her way and would have horrible nightmares. She would still have the nightmares from time to time, but now she played with the other children and she was always laughing and smiling. She still did not talk much, but considering everything that she had been through, her new state of mind was remarkable.

Later on that day, Kathrin was sitting in the living room playing with Isabel, her foster sister. She was trying her hardest not to mess her dress up. It was her favorite outfit, and when Ms. Walker said she could choose what she wanted to wear to meet the people who wanted to be her new mommy and daddy, she didn't have to think long about what to choose. Every time she put the dress on, she felt like a princess. She hoped her new parents would like her and think she looked like a princess too. She didn't want to do anything to upset them, and she told herself if they adopted her, she would always be good so they would never have a reason to give her back to her other family. Kathrin tried to block them out of her young, fragile mind, and most of the time she succeeded. Ms. Walker told her that they were bad people and that her new family would treat her good and love her like mommies and daddies are supposed to. She was very excited and could hardly wait for them to arrive.

"Kat."

Kathrin turned her head around so fast that her two long ponytails swung widely.

She saw Ms. Walker standing in the doorway, her greying hair wrapped up into a bun. A wide grin spread across her slightly wrinkled brown face as she made her announcement.

"Kathrin, I have some people I want you to meet, baby!"

She stepped to the side and there was a handsome couple standing side by side holding hands. They both looked down at Kathrin with beautiful smiles and love in their eyes. They had seen pictures of Kathrin, but they still weren't prepared for how beautiful she was. Her long wavy hair was pulled back into two ponytails that went past the middle of her back. Her eyes were an almond shape and were the color hazel. It seemed her skin had a glow to it. The mother, Vivian, knew at first sight that Kathrin would be a part of their family. She also knew that Kathrin came with a lot of baggage. It was hard to believe someone could do such a thing to a child, and Vivian's heart went out to her. She had to resist the urge to run to Kathrin and scoop her up in her arms and hold her like a baby.

"Are you my new mommy and daddy?" Kathrin asked as she looked into Vivian's eyes.

It was quiet in the room. Robert watched as his wife slowly walked to Kathrin, then dropped to her knees and put both of Kathrin's hands in hers.

"If you would like that, then yes, I would love to be your mother!" Vivian's voice was cracking as she fought back tears of joy.

She was finally going to have the daughter she always wanted.

CHAPTER 3

Kathrin loved her new family. She and Vivian spent lots of time together. They would go shopping and to the park. Vivian picked Kathrin up every day from private school, and on the weekends once a month, the whole family would take day trips to Disneyland, Knott's Berry Farm, SeaWorld, and the Zoo. Kathrin was experiencing things she never dreamed of, yet as an only child, she sometimes felt lonely. Both of her parents worked. Vivian was a professor at Cal State Long Beach and her father was a contractor.

As the years went by, Kat grew more beautiful and her young body began to transform into a woman's. Boys at her high school were going crazy over her, but she mostly shied away from them. She still had a deep distrust for men. It took her a long time to get close to her father, and she still found herself a little uncomfortable when she was alone in his presence, even though she knew how much he loved her. As she got older, she had also learned that men were easily controlled and would do just about anything for a beautiful and sexy woman. With this newfound power and all the free time she had with two working parents, she began to venture out into the world. Then when she was seventeen, she met T-Mack and her whole world changed.

One day Kat was shopping at the Fox Hills Mall with her home girl Sunshine. They were coming out of Victoria's Secret with bags in both hands, both dressed to impress. Kat was 5'4" and 120 pounds in all the right places -- round ass, not too big though, with nice hips, a small waist and a 36C cup breast size. She had it going on, to say the least. She loved the attention the fellas gave her. That was one of the reasons she had started waitressing at Stars with Sunshine just last month. She did not need the money, as she had a gold visa card that her dad paid off for her every month, as well as the allowance her parents still gave her every week, but she loved the attention she got from the guys at the club. She knew they didn't give a fuck about her, but it still made her feel good. The extra money was great too; she would go shopping almost every day of the week. Guys would stop her left and right. She would get nearly 20 numbers a day, but she would never call any of them. Sometimes she would see a guy who gave her his number weeks ago and she would not even remember him. She would make up an excuse as to why she never called and promise to call later.

This particular day was different though. When she and Sunshine came out of Victoria's Secret, she dropped one of her bags. Before she could retrieve it from the floor, T-Mack had picked it up with one hand while talking on the phone with the other. He handed it back, looked at her and smiled. Then he walked away before she could say thank you. She was stunned that he did not try to talk to her or get her number -- or give her his. This had never happened to her before. Maybe he was gay, she thought.

As soon as she walked away, Sunshine turned to Kat and said, "That nigga got it going on! Did you see his watch, girl? That Breitling cost like fifteen stacks. And his Franco chain looked heavy as fuck. I could tell, girl, cause those light ass hollow ones be swinging back and forth too much. You know I know my shit."

Kat just laughed and said, "Where you learn all that at, gold digging 101?"

"Whatever girl i saw your little hot ass checking him out. Don't even front, Plus the nigga fine as hell. He look like Reggie Bush, just lighter."

"Reggie who?" Kat asked, confused.

"Reggie the football player."

"You watch football?"

"Hell yes, girl. How else you goanna know a real baller when you see one? I watch basketball and baseball. You better get with the program, girl."

"You crazy, Sunshine!"

"Let's go to BJ's and get something to eat, bitch, while I put you up on game. It's about time you get a nigga. You the only virgin I know working at a strip club, bitch."

"I ain't no virgin bitch."

"You sure act like one. Niggas be trying to spend big money on yo little tight eye ass and you won't even do a lap dance for god's sake. You could be making a G a day!"

Kat hated when she made fun of her eyes, but decided to let it go. "I'm not in it for the money. I just like being at the club, that's all."

Sunshine just shook her head and laughed. She couldn't figure Kat out. They had met four months ago at the Beverly Center in the Louis Vuitton store. They were looking at the same bag and started talking. They had a lot in common and Sunshine said she had a friend that could get real Louis and Gucci bags sometimes for the low, so they exchanged numbers and before you knew it they were hanging out all the time. Sunshine always had money and was always wearing designer clothes, the latest this and that. But she was never at work and always had time to do things, so Kat asked her how this was possible. That's when she decided to put her up on game.

Sunshine was 24 years old and had been stripping for seven years, ever since she was seventeen, Kat's age. She told her she could get her a job if she wanted. At first Kat was reluctant, but then she said she would try it out once just to see if she could do it. She was an instant hit. All the brothers loved for her to wait on them. Kat had been working on the weekends for a month now.

They stepped into BJ's. It smelled good inside with all the different food cooking and being served. This was one of their favorite spots. They would eat there at least three times a week. It was attached right to the mall so you could shop till you dropped and then grab a bite to eat, and the food was really good. It was a little slow at lunchtime, so they were seated right away. As soon as they got to their table, Sunshine got excited.

"Girl don't look up, but Reggie Bush is sitting at the table behind us to the left."

Kat looked confused. "The football player?"

"The lookalike from the mall!"

Kat turned around and there he was with some guy, a big dark-skinned man that looked like a bouncer or a bodyguard. It looked as if they were talking about something important. They both had serious looks on their faces and the big guy kept shaking his head no. T-Mack looked irritated. He pulled a white envelope from his jacket pocket and slid it across the table. The other man opened it up and looked inside. Then he smiled and put the envelope in his pocket. They both stood up and shook hands. Then the big guy walked away.

T-Mack sat back down and that's when he noticed the girls. He saw Kat try to turn away as if she wasn't looking, but it was too late. She was busted.

T-Mack got up and walked over to their table and introduced himself. "Hello ladies. Didn't I see you two in the mall earlier?"

They both smiled and said yes.

"Well, my boy had to leave and I hate eating alone, so would you mind if I joined you at your table? I mean, unless you were expecting someone else. You know, like a boyfriend. I wouldn't want to get you ladies in trouble. By the way, my name is Travon."

He held his hand out to Kat. She shook it and tried to pull it away, but he held on for a second and then let go as she began to talk.

"No, we were not expecting anyone. It's just me and my girl, Sun... I mean Meka. We just finished shopping and were just going to grab something to eat."

"Hello? Kat's not the only one here."

T-Mack turned and looked at Sunshine. "Excuse me. I'm so sorry, ma. How could I miss you?"

He shook her hand and sat down next to Kat.

"My name's Meka and this my girl Kat. So what kind of work you do? And please don't say you a street pharmacist, because it seem like that's all niggas is doing these days. It pays good, but the vacations are a little too long for me, if you know what I mean."

Mack started laughing. "Naw, ma. It ain't like that. I don't sell no drugs. Why every time a brother looking like he got his shit together, he got to be slanging dope? You worse than one time."

Then he did his cop impression. "Are you on probation or parole? Please step out of the car. You got any guns or narcotics on you?"

"So what you do then?" Sunshine asked again.

Kat could tell Sunshine was starting to get an attitude because Travon wasn't paying her any attention. He seemed to be focused on her, and Sunshine hated when Kat got more attention. Sunshine was 5'8" with a D cup breast size. She wore a long blond weave to her ass, which matched her light brown skin. That's how she got the name Sunshine. She had an ass so big, you could set drinks on it. Niggas loved her ass. Her face was average, but her ass made up for that. See in the hood, a black women's ass was like a white women's breast in the suburbs. It made all the difference. Any time a brother gave Kat too much attention, Sunshine would get jealous. That was one thing Kat didn't like about her.

The waitress, a tall, light-skinned black girl, brought the girls their drinks and asked if they were ready to order. Would Mack be dining with them, she wondered? He told her he was, and they all placed their orders. When she left, they started their conversation back up.

"Well, I'm actually a boxer training at Venice Beach right now," Mack explained.

It was really the truth, except he wasn't a pro and he wasn't getting paid. He was not about to tell them that he robbed people for a living, however. That was not the best icebreaker.

"So you a boxer like Mike Tyson?" Kat felt stupid the minute the words came out of her mouth, but she felt she had to say something to direct the conversation back to her.

But Mike Tyson? Was that the only boxer she could think of? Did he even still box? Fortunately, Mack just smiled and looked her in the eyes as if he was trying to read her mind. There was something about him that was so attractive. Yeah, he looked good. The brother was fine, but it was more than that. It was the way he carried himself with such confidence, not really cockiness, but like he knew where he was going in life and what he wanted out of it. She was really feeling him and she could tell he was feeling her too.

"Yeah, ma. You could say that. But I'm just starting out, so I wouldn't compare myself to him just yet."

"So where is your next fight?" Kat asked.

He thought about it for a minute. He hated lying too much, so he just told the truth.

"I don't have a fight for a while, but I'm sparring against a guy out of Vegas next week. If you want, you guys can come."

"I think I'll pass on that, rookie," Sunshine said.

But he really wasn't talking to her. He wasn't even looking in her direction. He was gazing at Kat the whole time.

"I think I want to come," Kat said, trying to match his gaze but failing. "Give me your number and I will stop by if I have time."

She pulled out her smart phone and he gave her the number. Their food arrived. They ate and continued talking.

Kat and T-Mack were really feeling each other. She couldn't remember the last time she was interested in a guy this much. An hour went by and everyone had finished eating. The waitress came by with the check and put it on the table.

T-Mack picked it up, put a hundred dollar bill in the checkbook and handed it back to her. "Keep the change, ma!"

Both girls were impressed, as their meals only came up to $15 dollars each. They stood up to leave. They had parked on the other side of the mall. T-Mack had parked right in front of BJ's, so he offered them a ride to their car.

As they walked out, he carried Kat's bags. They walked through the parking lot and stopped at the back of a black S55 Benz on 22" black and silver forged rims. He dug into his pocket with his free hand and popped the trunk to place Kat's bags inside. Then he took Sunshine's and did the same with hers.

While he was busy in the trunk, Sunshine looked at Kat and gave her the thumbs up. Kat rolled her eyes at her, but she couldn't help being a little impressed. She could tell Mack was getting money, but she didn't know if she bought the whole boxer thing. He did offer for them to come see him fight, so maybe he really was a boxer, however. She really didn't know, but what she did know was that she would be calling him.

They all got in and T-Mack drove through the parking lot across the mall to Sunshine's car. He got out, grabbed their bags from the truck and handed them to the girls.

"And by the way, how old are you, girl?"

Kat looked at him for a minute, thinking before she responded. She didn't want to say 17 and scare him away. Even though most niggas wouldn't care, he seemed different. She would be 18 in a few months, so what the hell was the difference anyway, she thought?

"I am 18. How old are you?"

"I just turned 21. You know I want to hear from you before the fight. You can hit me any time," he said with that smile she was beginning to love.

She smiled right back and said, "Ok, I'll do that."

Then she turned and walked towards Sunshine's car, putting extras on her already sexy walk. She knew he would be watching her, and when she turned to get in the car, he was still standing there watching her every move just like she knew he would be. Kat waved as she got in, then he got in his car and drove off.

As soon as they were alone, Sunshine started in on her. "Girl, that nigga was all up in your face, bitch, and the brother is paid! Did you see that nigga's car? I was ready to suck his fucking dick right they're in front of you girl when I saw that Benz. The nigga is a fucking boxer. You hit the jackpot, bitch. Please tell me you don't want him, because if you don't, I will definitely take him off your hands."

Kat just shook her head. She knew Sunshine wasn't playing. The bitch was a gold digger in every sense of the word. As they drove up Slauson, Kat was looking out the window.

She turned to Sunshine. "I think I really like him, Meka. He seemed different than all the other niggas in LA that be trying to get your number as soon as they see you. I mean, when he first saw us in the mall, he didn't even sweat us. That shit don't ever happen to us. I think I'm going to call him tonight."

"Damn, girl. Look at you. It's about time you stop acting like a nun and get some dick, bitch. You know I was just playing about taking him off your hands. You know I don't get down like that."

"Yeah, I know. Plus you already got a man, and I don't think Gee's crazy ass would go for that shit," she said laughing.

"Girl, please. Gee's ass is pussy-whipped. My nigga does whatever I say. He just be trying to front in front of people, but he know who really runs the show. Pussy trumps dick any day. You feel me?"

Both girls laughed and high-fived, then Sunshine dropped Kat off in front of her house. Kat went inside and put her bags in her room, then into the living room to watch TV. Her parents didn't get home until around six. She graduated in June from high school and was going to Cal State LA in the fall, so for now there wasn't much to do besides shop, work at the club, watch TV and eat. She tried not to do too much of the latter, and nothing good was on TV, so she turned TiVo on to watch some old episodes of the Bad Girls Club. She looked at her phone and thought about calling Travon, but she knew it was too soon. He would probably think she was sweating him, but she just could not stop thinking about him. She found herself picking up her phone and looking up his number. Then she put it down.

"No," she told herself.

It was too soon. She would call him tomorrow. Yeah, that's what she would do. Give it a day or two. Well, maybe not two.

She picked the phone back up and texted her girl Kim from school. "Guess what, bitch?"

Chapter 4

Later on that night in Hollywood, Mack was sitting in the parking lot of Club Voodoo on Hollywood and Vine in a Range Rover that he rented from Custom Rentals in Beverly Hills. He was waiting for the club to close at 2 am. His boys Lil Man and Booboo were waiting in a G-ride three blocks away. They were two young grimy niggas from Santana Block, Crips out of Compton, California, that he knew through his cousin Solo. Lil Man and Booboo were always down to get paid; it didn't matter what they had to do as long as there was money involved. Mack was a Blood, but money was all he cared about. He didn't give a fuck where you were from, as long as you were down to get paid. That was all that mattered.

As he sat in the truck waiting, he could hear the music from two different clubs. The parking lot was packed and there were people walking around everywhere. He rolled up the windows and pushed play on his iPod. Ms. Keys came on.

I was wondering maybe... Could I make you my baby...

He couldn't help but think about the girl he'd met earlier that day at BJ's. He wished he would have gotten her number. She was fine as hell. He had never been with an Asian girl before. He thought that's what she was, but you could tell she had some black in her. She could pass for Hawaiian, too. Shit, he didn't know what she was. All he knew was that she had been on his mind all day and he couldn't even call her because he hadn't even gotten her phone number. Not that he would have called her on the first day. She probably would have thought he was a square. He never called a girl on the first night. He always waited a few days. But he guessed that didn't matter, because he didn't have her number. He would just have to wait for her to call him. He wasn't dating anyone at the time and he was tired of the females that he had been fucking with lately. They seemed to all be the same and he was looking for something else -- something different. Yeah, Kat was definitely different. Maybe she was just what he was looking for.

The passenger door suddenly swung open, catching him off guard. He reached on the side of his seat for his Glock, but it was too late. A huge, dark-skinned guy was already in the passenger seat pointing something in his face.

"Oh shit," he thought.

Then he saw the man's face. It was the same man from BJ's, his cousin Solo. He had his cell phone in his hand and was pointing it at Mack as if it was a gun. Then he started laughing.

"You should have seen your face, blood. You looked all fucked up! Ha ha! Like you was about to shit on yourself, my nigga. You slippin', dawg. How you gonna let a nigga get up on you like that? You supposed to be a mutha fuckin' jack artist."

He was still laughing hard, but Mack didn't see anything funny about it. He was pissed off.

"Man, ain't nobody got time for your stupid ass games, blood. You lucky I knew it was you, cause your brains was about to be on your lap, nigga. So you need to stall that shit out!"

"Calm down, Mack. You know ya boy was just fucking with you."

"Yeah whatever, man. So did you handle everything?"

"Yeah, dawg. I gave the bitch the money earlier and she said she's gonna text me when they done collecting the money. They don't count it, she said. They just throw it in a big bag and walk out the side door over there." Solo pointed to a door on the side of the club about 100 feet across the parking lot. "They put it in the trunk of that grey Audi truck. He likes to leave right after closing, so they blend in with all the traffic leaving the club, so you got to stay on them. The owner is a tall Persian dude with long black hair and the girl is a skinny blond with big tits. She got on a black dress tonight. I haven't seen the dude, but he don't never come out the office and I only work the door and VIP, so I don't got clearance to go back there."

Mack was listening to his cousin talk, going over everything in his mind to make sure he hadn't missed anything.

"Yeah and the rest is on y'all, man," Solo said as he glanced at his watch. "What the fuck is you listening to? Don't tell me you done fucked around and fell in love, blood?"

"Whatever, man. Don't even front like you don't listen to this shit," Mack said, as he pushed pause on his iPod.

"Yeah, when I'm with a bitch," Solo replied. "I see why you was slippin earlier, you done fucked around and feel in love and shit."

Solo was laughing again. The nigga thought he had jokes. Then all of a sudden the club started letting out. Women and men were coming out and walking to their cars. Some were leaving and some stuck around talking to each other. Others looked too drunk to be driving.

"Damn, did you see the ass on that white bitch right there, blood? I got to go get that," Solo said as he got out of the truck. "Hey girl, hold up for a minute."

Mack just shook his head. His cousin was a real cock hound. He kept his eyes on the door and the gray Audi truck. He was not about to let Solo fuck this up. The nigga was tripping. Out there trying to get a number while he was supposed to be waiting on a text message.

His cousin walked back to the Range Rover window, motioning for Mack to roll it down. "The bitch just hit me. They should be coming out in five minutes, so handle your business, blood. I gotta go back in the club. Hit me when y'all done and I will see you tomorrow, alright?"

"Don't trip. I got this. I'll holla at you later." Mack picked up the phone and called Lil Man.

"Yeah, hello?" Lil Man answered.

"It's me, Mack. Y'all niggas ready?"

"Hell yeah, cuz. Me and Booboo waiting on you."

"Well they coming out right now, so go to the 7-Eleven and when you see a gray Audi truck drive by with a silver Range Rover behind it, fall in behind us. We will be headed for the 101 Freeway. Soon as we get close to the freeway, get in front of us and you know the rest, right?"

"Yeah, cuz. We got it. We on our way right now."

"Alright, my nigga." Mack hung up the phone.

The parking lot was getting empty. He hoped they hurried up and came out before he was the only other vehicle out there. He was looking at the door when it finally swung open. The hatch back popped up on the Audi truck at the same time and a tall white guy came out carrying a nice-sized duffle bag. He threw it in the back and slammed the door closed, then jumped in and started the truck up. The blond lady finally came out and got in. It was just like his cuzzo said it would be. They drove past Mack and turned left out the parking lot onto Vine headed north. Mack started up the double RR and followed them, staying one car behind.

They were coming up by the 7-Eleven now. Mack looked in the parking lot and saw the black Lincoln Town Car with its right turn signal on getting ready to pull out into traffic. As he passed in front of the car, he could see Lil Man behind the wheel and Booboo on the passenger side. They turned into traffic, changed lanes, and then pulled right behind the Range Rover. All three vehicles made the next light. Then the Town Car changed lanes and sped up. Lil Man and Booboo were making their move. They passed T-Mack, then the Audi. As soon as they had made it past the next light, the Lincoln swerved in front of the motorcade. The last light was coming up and they needed it to turn red, so they slowed down the car a bit. The light turned yellow and they slowed to a stop. The Audi blew its horn, but it was too late. The light had turned red.

Mack pulled the Range Rover all the way up to the bumper of the Audi, boxing it in between him and the Lincoln. Both doors on the Town Car flew open. Lil Man and Booboo came running out with blue rags tied over their faces and ski caps pulled down to their eyes. Both had their guns drawn. Lil Man ran to the back window and broke the glass with the butt of his gun. The whole window shattered. Booboo reached in and grabbed the bag while Lil Man watched his back.

They could hear the club owner shouting at them. "What the fuck? Hey, stop. What the fuck are you doing? Put that bag down now!"

Then there was a big explosion and a flash inside the Audi.

BAM.

"Oh shit. This fool busting on us," Booboo said.

Lil Man turned around, pointed his TEC-9 and opened fire.

POP POP POP POP POP.

He let off five shots, hitting the driver's side door and shattering the window. The blond lady was screaming at the top of her lungs. Booboo had made it back to the Town Car with the bag.

He turned and yelled to Lil Man, "Let's go, cuz. One time is on their way!"

You could hear sirens coming from a distance. Cars were honking their horns and swerving around them, some not even aware of what was going on. Lil Man ran by the driver's door of the Audi and the owner fired his gun again.

BAM BAM!

He barely missed Lil Man's head.

Lil Man ducked down, turned around and opened fire on the driver's side door again.

POP POP POP POP POP POP!

This time he unloaded the rest of the 30-round clip. Then Booboo opened fire at the windshield, unloading his 10-shot 45.

BAM BAM BAM BAM!

Lil Man finally made it to the Lincoln. They climbed in and pulled off, burning rubber and running a red light while almost getting sideswiped by another car.

Back in the Range Rover, Mack could hear the sirens getting closer. He backed the truck up and drove around the Audi. As he sped up, he could see two bodies sprawled across the front seats. Blood was all over the place. The blond lady's hair was covered with it. He thought he might have seen her brains splattered across the dashboard.

T-Mack got on the 101 South doing a hundred until he caught up with the Town Car. He flashed his high beams and the Town Car pulled over to the shoulder. Mack pulled over behind them. Lil Man and Booboo jumped out and ran to the passenger side of T-Mack's truck. Lil Man got in the front and Booboo got in the back with the bag on his lap.

"Damn, that fool tried to blow my head off."

"Yeah, nigga. All I heard was *BAM!* Then I turned around and started getting off. This TEC-9 ain't no joke. I lit that white boy's ass up!" Lil Man was laughing, but Mack could tell he was shook up.

They had just killed two people and if they got caught, their lives would be over. Double murder gets you the death penalty in Cali. He really didn't know if he wanted to put his life in these two niggas' hands. He really didn't know them like that. All it would take was one of them to tell one person and it would all go bad.

"Yeah, you did that, cuzz. That's why I had to get off with my 45. I couldn't let you have all the fun. You see the way that bitch's head exploded? That shit looked crazy!" Booboo chimed in.

Mack said, "Yeah, y'all did good, my niggas we in the clear now. So just sit back and relax. We should be at the spot in 20 minutes so we can count this cash."

Then he noticed blood on Lil Man's face.

"Hey, nigga, is that your blood?" He pointed at Lil Man's face.

Lil Man touched his face and looked at his hand.

"Damn, I didn't even notice I was bleeding," he said, still staring at all the blood on his hand. "I must have got hit by some glass."

And just like that, Mack knew what he had to do.

"Don't even trip. You can get cleaned up at the spot. I kept extra clothes over there". "Good looking, my nigga." Mack turned the music up and leaned back.

Ten minutes later they got on the 110 South. They drove a while, and then exited on Imperial. They made a right, and then went south on Figueroa, driving a few blocks. They passed Rosecrans, entering the industrial part of

Compton. It was just factories and auto repair shops. Mack turned onto a small street, pulled over and turned the car off. Lil Man and Booboo were looking around confused, wondering why they were there.

"What the fuck is over here, cuzz?" Lil Man asked.

"We got to switch cars again. I can't let know anyone by my spot see us in this truck, so grab the money and let's go. My Benz is down the street." Mack took the keys out of the ignition and exited the vehicle.

Booboo grabbed the money, and then he and Lil Man both got out on the passenger side. It was dark on the street and there was only one streetlight on. You could hear dogs barking far away. The only other sound was the freeway off in the distance. Mack came around the back of the truck and stood on the sidewalk with the other two.

"We gotta walk down this way around the corner," he said, pointing down the street.

They all took off walking in the direction he indicated.

"This bag is heavy as fuck. We couldn't drive?"

As Mack stopped to tie his shoe, the other two passed him by. Then with one swift motion, he stood up, pulled his gun out and shot Booboo once in the back of the head. His lifeless body hit the ground like a ton of bricks.

Lil Man's eyes got big. He turned and tried to reach for Mack's Glock, but it was too late. Mack squeezed the trigger twice and two bullets tore into the side of Lil Man's face, killing him instantly.

Mack pulled the duffel bag out of Booboo's lifeless hands and ran back to the truck. He got in and started it back up, peeling off. He drove up one block to El Segundo and got on the 110 North heading home. He wiped his gun off as he drove, and then threw it out the window before he got off the freeway.

T-Mack pulled through the gated entrance of his apartment complex. The guard was asleep in the gatehouse like always. For $2500 a month, you think you would get better security, but apparently not. He pulled the truck around and drove into the underground parking lot. He parked next to his Benz. He was home free. He grabbed the duffel bag and his keys, got out, then walked to the elevator and pushed the button. The doors opened instantly and he stepped in and pushed the button for the 3rd floor.

He entered the dimly lit house. The only light came from a 200-gallon saltwater tank in the living room. He stepped in, closed the door and deactivated the alarm. He then walked past a small dining room and entered the living room. He turned the lights on and sat down on his off-white leather couch. He then sat the bag down at his feet and reached for the remote. He turned the 80-inch flat screen TV on over his fireplace. A rerun of MTV's "Cribs" was on.

He stared at the bag and couldn't help feeling bad about what happened to his boys. Still, he knew he really didn't have a choice. He had to take care of Lil Man and Booboo because for one, he didn't know if he could trust them to keep their mouths shut. All it would take was for one of them to tell one person and he just didn't know if he could trust them. Even if he could, it really didn't matter. Once the cops found the stolen car with Lil Man's blood all over it, they would be all over their Asses. He couldn't let that happen.

He got up, walked to the kitchen and grabbed a glass out of the dishwasher. Then he opened up the fridge and grabbed a bottle of Grey Goose. He walked back to the living room, sat back down and poured himself a shot. He set the bottle down on the coffee table and took a drink.

"That's better," he thought.

He reached for the duffel bag, pulled it In front of him and unzipped it. He couldn't believe his eyes.

"Damn." He turned the bag over and dumped the money on the floor.

Rolls of rubber banded 100's, 50's, 20's, 10's, 5's, and 1's fell out onto the floor. There had to be close to $200K. He just stared at it. His cousin had said that the club was making money and he knew that it had a 2000-person capacity and all the money from the bar, but he was not expecting this much money. He was thinking maybe $80K or a $100K tops. He jumped up and ran to his bedroom. He came back out with a white shoebox. He opened it up and pulled his money counter out. He took another sip of vodka and grabbed a roll of hundreds. This was going to take a minute.

Chapter 5

Kat had just finished eating a sandwich for lunch and was about to get in the shower. She had gotten home from the club at 2:30 in the morning and gone straight to bed. She woke up at 12:30 in the afternoon and the first thing she did was to pick up the phone. She pulled Travon's number up. She was about to call him, but decided to wait a minute, eat and get dressed first.

As she stripped down and got in the shower, she kept replaying every word that was said between them the day before in her mind. The way he looked at her, the way he smiled, the way he laughed -- it was all so sexy. There was something about him that she was very attracted to. She thought it was a little silly feeling this way about someone she had just met, but she couldn't help it. She was smiling just thinking about him.

She turned off the water and stepped out, grabbed the towel and walked into her bedroom, drying herself off. She went to her dresser and pulled out some Hello Kitty boy shorts and a tank top and slid them on. Then she sat on the bed and wrapped the towel around her head so her hair could finish drying.

"What the hell," she thought.

She picked up the phone and dialed his number. It rang five times. She was about to hang up when his voice came through the phone.

"You know who you called, so leave a message and I'll get back to you."

"Ummmm…. This is Kat. We met yesterday at BJ's. I was about to go grab something to eat, so call me if you want to join me. My number is 310-777-6161. Ok, bye." She hung up the phone.

"Damn," she thought.

She wasn't expecting his voicemail. She wasn't prepared to leave a message, so she just said the first thing that came to her mind. Of course, she had just finished eating so it didn't make sense.

"Get something to eat? Oh well. He probably will take a minute to call back and I could just say he took too long and I ate already and we could do something else if he wants," she thought.

"Yeah, that will work."

Then the phone rang. She looked at the caller ID and it was him. She cleared her throat with an "Umm umm" then answered the phone.

"Hello?"

"What up, ma. This Travon."

"I know who this is. What you doing?"

"Nothing much, girl, Just about to head to my relative house. I got your message. Where you trying to go eat at?"

"It don't matter. I was bored and figured I would go eat. I just got up not too long ago."

"You bored, huh? So that's the only reason you hit me ma? Damn, I thought maybe I was on your mind. Cause you been on my mind all day."

"No, it's not even like that, boy. I have been thinking about you a little. That's why I called."

Kathrin couldn't believe what she had just heard. He had been thinking about her too!

"Boy? A little? You know I'm a grown man, right? I stopped playing in the sandbox a long time ago."

"You funny," she said, laughing.

"I'm glad I could make you laugh, ma. But on a serious note, I'm glad you called. You have been on my mind, and that ain't no cap. I know niggas be on yo ass."

"I know bitches be on you, too. You probably got like 10, huh. And don't lie," she said with a giggle so she wouldn't let on as to how important the question really was.

"Naw girl, it ain't even like that. I really don't have time for a relationships, so I don't have no one right now."

"Whatever boy, that's what they all say."

"That's real, ma. I'm not trying to run no game. Females these days got too much baggage. Baby daddies and all that, I really don't need the dram."

"Is that right? But what about you? Do you got any rug rats running around?"

Please don't let him have no kids, she thought.

"Naw, babe. I don't have no young yet. I haven't found the right women. I see how some of you females act once you get pregnant." He was laughing.

"That's because niggas be trifling. But anyways, were you stay at?"

"I live over in Westchester by Friday's. Why? You going to come clean my house?"

"If you were my man I would, but since we just met, I'm going to have to pass."

They continued to joke back and forth.

"So you clean for your man, huh. Do you cook, too?"

"I sure do. My dad taught me how."

"Your dad? Why not your mom?" T-Mack was a little confused.

"Please. My mom hardly ever cook," she said laughing.

The conversation went on for an hour. She really enjoyed talking to him. He made her laugh a lot. It was like she had known him for a while. She could have stayed on the phone with him all day.

Then his line began to beep.

"Hold on." He clicked over for a second, then came back.

"Hello?"

"Yeah, I'm still here," she answered.

"That was my relative. I didn't realize how long we were on the phone."

"I'm sorry," Kat replied.

"Naw, don't trip. I enjoyed it, but I gotta go meet him."

"Well, you can call me later," she said, feeling a little disappointed that their conversation was about to come to an end.

"I was gonna ask if you wanted to come with me. I just got to stop by his house real fast, then we can go get something to eat."

"Sure," she said, feeling happy now that she knew she was going to see him.

She gave him the address.

"Ok, I'll be there in fifteen minutes."

"Alright. Bye."

She hung up the phone and jumped off the bed. She had to hurry up and find something to wear. Kathrin ran to the closet and found a light blue pair of Seven jeans. She pulled them on. They fit just right, tightly hugging her body like a glove. She took her tank top off and put on a lace bra. Now all she needed was a shirt. She looked through her dresser and found a black BeBe tank top and some black and gray open toe stilettoes. Then she went in the bathroom, brushed her long black hair into a ponytail, put on some Bobbi Brown lip-gloss, a little eyeliner and some blush. She checked herself out in the mirror. She really wasn't satisfied, but it would have to do because she didn't have time to change. He would be there any minute and she didn't want to keep him waiting. She grabbed her Prada purse and shades off the dresser and went downstairs to wait.

Chapter 6

T-Mack turned off of Crenshaw on to 79th. He went north three blocks, and then pulled over in front of Kat's house.

"You have arrived at your destination," the navigation system informed him.

He picked his phone up and called her.

"Hello?" Kat answered.

"I'm outside. You ready?"

"Yeah, I'll be out right now."

He hung up the phone and looked around. It was a nice neighborhood. The houses were two stories and the lawns were well manicured. There wasn't one person outside and it was 3: pm in the afternoon. There were lots of trees and you could hear birds chirping. He definitely was not on the Eastside. If he had been, there would have been at least twenty people walking around outside.

A door opened from a two-story brown house with white trimming. Kat stepped out with her shades on looking all Hollywood. She locked the door behind her and walked to the car. He unlocked the doors so she could get in. He looked at her and she seemed more beautiful now than when they first met. She was beyond fine. He had been with a lot of females, but she took the cake.

"So you going to sit there and stare at me or you gonna give me a hug or something?"

She took her shades off and put them on her head, looking at him with those beautiful light brown eyes. He wanted to lean over and kiss her so he could feel her little soft-looking lips, but decided against it and went with the hug. When he reached over and wrapped his strong muscular arms around her petite frame, he could smell her perfume and the shampoo in her hair. When he released her, she was smiling.

"That's more like it. So where your cousin live?"

As he turned the Benz around, he finally found his voice.

"He stay on Fig and 91st. We'll be there in a second."

She was looking around the car. It was roomie inside and very quiet. You couldn't hear a thing outside. She looked at the touchscreen navigation system and hit the iPod symbol. A music list popped up and she scrolled down to Lloyd and skipped through the tracks till she found one she liked.

"Ha. Hazel." He was glancing out the corner of his eye, surprised she knew how to work the system.

"I see you made yourself at home," he smiled. "I guess you been in some nice rides. You seem to know your way around."

"My dad has the same kind of stereo in his Jag."

"Yeah? What does he do?"

"He's a contractor and my mom is a professor at Cal State Long Beach. So we do alright."

"I see. You got any sisters or brothers?"

"Yeah, I got a brother, but he don't live with us. He's twenty-four." She sat back and turned Lloyd up.

I think I'm in love…I'm in love…

They drove up Manchester just listening to music, enjoying each other's company. He caught her texting on her phone a few times, but it didn't really bother him. Everyone did it these days. Plus she was responding to texts, not sending them.

He turned on Fig. There were prostitutes on almost every corner. They glared at his ride as he sped past them. Kat glazed out the window at the prostitutes and smokers and felt bad for them. She wished there was something she could do to help, but knew firsthand life was not fair. She looked at Mack and turned the music down as he made a left on 91st.

"You ever feel like you should be doing more with your life?" She paused, trying to figure out the right way to express what she was thinking. "You know, something to change the way things are?"

"Wow, girl. Where did all that come from? You going all philosophical on me?"

He was laughing as he pulled into the driveway of a brown house with a Dodge Charger on 24" rims in the driveway. He honked the horn.

"Don't laugh at me, Travon. I'm serious. That's the last time I will try to get deep with you." She started pouting, but he thought it was cute.

"I was playing, girl. Don't be mad. You just caught me off guard, ma. But to answer your question, I believe in helping yourself. See, if everyone took care of their own -- like if I have kids, I'm gonna take care of them and raise them right so they not running the streets and being manic and all -- if everyone did that, the world would be a better place."

She was about to comment when the bar doors opened up on the house they were parked at. Mack's cousin Solo walked out to the car.

"What up, my boy?"

"You my nigga, that's what's up!"

"Damn, nigga, what do you have here?" Solo was looking Kat up and down.

"Kat, this is my cousin Solo. Solo, Kat."

"Hi," she waved at him.

"Damn, you fine. You got a sister or what?"

He made her blush. She was feeling a little embarrassed at the way he complemented her, even though she really loved the attention.

"Naw, dawg. She don't got no sister. But if you want, I can see what's up with her brother."

"Real funny, blood."

Mack got out of the car laughing and grabbed a Louis Vuitton backpack off the back seat. "I will be right back, ma."

"Ok."

They walked inside the house. Inside there was an old lady on the couch watching Wheel of Fortune on TV. Mack said hi as he walked by her headed for the back room. Solo opened the door to the room and both men went in.

"Lock the door behind you, dawg."

"Man, what the fuck happened, nigga? All hell broke loose last night. One time was all over the place. They held all the staff till like five in the morning asking all kind of questions and shit. Then I tried to call Lil Man and one time picked up his phone so I hung up and call Booboo. I get the same pig on the line, so I call yo ass."

Solo was staring at T-Mack, waiting for an explanation.

"Man, the shit hit the fan, blood. And your boys aired it out," he said real calm.

"That's it?"

"Pretty much. I mean, I don't think you need the play-by-play. Besides, this is for you," Mack threw him the Louie bag.

Solo caught it and opened it up, then smiled. "That's what I'm talking about. This the whole 25 thousand?"

"Naw, I put a little extra."

"How much extra?"

Solo started taking the money out of the bag. He shook it upside down, making sure he got it all. Then he threw it back to Mack.

"25 thousand extra."

"Damn, how much did y'all pass for?" Solo knew it had to be a lot if Mack threw in an extra 25 thousand.

"Said you wanted 25 stacks. Well, that's 50, so it really don't matter what I get as long as we all happy, right?"

Mack got up and was getting ready to leave. He wasn't about to tell Solo how much he made cause he knew if his cousin knew his cut was 150 thousand, he would want a little more and that was not about to happen.

"Yeah, you right. But have you heard from Booboo and Lil Man? I think they got busted or something."

"I dropped them off at a room in Torrance, then went back home. But if one time's answering the niggas' phones, I wouldn't be calling them back if I was you."

"Yeah, you probably right. So what's up for the night? Dawg, let's hit the strip club or something," Solo said, counting his money.

"Boy, you see what I got out there? I'll holla at you tomorrow, blood. I'm out."

They gave each other some dap and Solo walked him to the front. He knew something was not right with Lil Man and Booboo, but knew better then to press the issue. He'd find out sooner rather than later.

Kat was talking on the phone with Sunshine when she saw Mack come out the door headed for the car.

"I gotta go, girl. He's coming."

"You coming to work later? Or you staying with that nigga?"

"It depends. I'll call you when he drops me off. Ok, bye."

She hung up the phone and looked in the mirror to make sure her make-up looked good. T-Mack opened the door and got in.

"Get out that mirror girl. You can't get no finer." He closed the mirror on her, smiling and shaking his head.

"Whatever, boy." She started playing with the stereo looking for another song. "So where are you taking me?"

"You eat seafood?"

"Yeah, I love it."

"Good. Me too. I might take you to one of my spots, McCormick and Schmicks. It's in Manhattan Beach. You been there before?"

"No, I don't think so. Me and my mom go out to eat a lot. Well, we use to, but I don't think I been there."

"What kind of places niggas be taking you?"

She found a song she liked, something slow by Ashanti.

"Well, I haven't really been on that many dates. I had a few boyfriends in high school, but they didn't really take me out to eat. We would usually go to the movies. You know, stuff like that."

"So you telling me a nigga ain't never took you out to eat?" He was staring at her with a look of disbelief.

"I just turned eighteen, Travon, so it shouldn't be that much of a shock." She paused, and then looked right at him, Ashanti still singing her heart-breaking love songs out of the speakers.

"How many girls have you taken here?"

"It ain't even like that. This ain't the type of joint you take any old body, so you don't have to worry about that. I usually come here with my family."

"So what you trying to say? I'm special or something?"

"Most definitely, Kathrin." He gazed in her eyes with an intense look. "You are something special. I know we just met and this is only our second date, but I know something special when I see it."

She turned away and stared out the window. The nigga was good. She knew he might be running game on her, but he damn near made her heart and pussy melt at the same time. She could feel her nipples get hard and he had not even touched her. She was gonna have to be careful around him if she wanted to keep her panties on tonight.

They got off the 405 Freeway on Rosecrans and drove west towards the beach. They got to an area with restaurants on both sides and a couple of movie theaters, then made a right onto a small street and pulled into valet parking. The valet opened Kat's door then came around and gave Mack his ticket and drove his car away. He walked to her, put his hand at the small of her back and guided her through the doors.

As he talked to the maître d', she looked around. The decor was really fancy. It looked expensive. She noticed there were not many black people. She looked at her clothes and felt a little out of place with jeans on, but Travon was dressed similarly. He had on black designer jeans, black and brown Nikes and a black and brown, flannel, long-sleeved, button-up shirt, a diamond chain and a platinum Rolex. He looked like a superstar.

"This way, please." A tall blond lady led them to a cozy table in the corner with a view of the Boulevard.

The waiter took their drink orders. They both ordered waters and Mack had them bring them a bottle of white wine. He came back and sat a silver bucket of ice on the table and showed Mack the bottle of wine for his approval. Mack shook his head yes and the waiter popped the cork and filled two glasses. He said he would be back shortly to take the orders.

"He didn't even ask you for your ID," Kat said, surprised.

"Well, in places like this they rarely do." He took a sip of his wine and sat it back down. "I'm sorry, ma. I didn't even ask you if you drink."

"It's ok," she said, taking a small sip. "I do sometimes. Some wines taste nasty, but I like this one."

"I'm glad you do. It's one of my favorites and you can only get it here or in France."

"Look at you boy. France. What you going tell me next, you been overseas?" She was laughing as she took another sip.

Mack started laughing too. "Naw babe, I ain't never been to France. The waiter told me once, that's all. But I would like to leave the States one day."

"Where to?"

He thought for a minute. "I don't know... Somewhere."

"Well, I want to go too. Italy or Spain." She started to reach for the bottle to pour herself another glass.

"Let me do that for you, babe. You gonna have these people thinking I don't have no manners."

She sat back and watched him pour the wine. He was always so nice to her. She wondered if it was all a front, but she hoped it wasn't. She really liked him, but she knew most men only wanted one thing and once they got it, everything changed. She didn't want to get her heart broken, but she couldn't help but being attracted to him.

The waiter came back and took their orders. Kat couldn't decide on what she wanted, so Mack ordered scallops and shrimp fettuccini and lobster fettuccini with two caesar salads. They sampled each other's food. Their conversation carried on through dinner as they talked about everything -- family, kids, things they wanted out of life. Two hours later, after they finished the whole bottle of wine, Mack paid the check and they walked outside to the front. The valet brought the car around. Kat was feeling good. She was tipsy and Mack had to help her get in the car. When he closed his door, he pulled off and headed to the freeway.

It was still early and Kat wasn't ready to go home.

"So what's up? You taking me home?"

She was looking at him, trying to judge his reaction to her question, but his expression never changed. He was always so cool. She could never tell what he was thinking.

"I got to meet my little bro at my house in a minuet, but if you want you can come with me."

"Yeah, that's cool because I'm not ready to go home yet. It's boring as hell at my house. My parents just watch TV and stay in their room."

Plus she was dying to see his house. Her mom always told her you could tell a lot about a man by his home and how he kept it. She wondered what Mack's house would say about him. He opened up the door, then let Kat in then turned the alarm off. The lights came on. He hardly ever brought girls to his house, just every once in a while. He knew the drama they could cause popping up and making a scene, plus he didn't trust anyone these days, so he chose carefully who he allowed to come over.

He turned the TV on and gave her the remote. "Make yourself at home. There's drinks in the fridge. I'll be right back."

He disappeared in the room. When he came back out, there was a bottle of Moet and two glasses of orange juice on the coffee table. She poured Champaign into the glasses and handed Mack one.

"I like your condo. I know you got a maid because it's way too clean."

He opened the patio doors, stepped outside and fired up a kush blunt. "Naw, ma. I ain't got no maid. I just keep my shit clean. I can't stand a messy house."

He hit the blunt a couple of times, then held it out to her. She got up off the couch with her glass in hand and walked to him. She had taken her heels off and left them by the door when she came in because she was afraid of getting the white carpet dirty, so now she was much shorter than him.

He looked down at her feet. They looked good. She had her toenails painted to match her fingernails and he couldn't help but wonder what she looked like with her clothes off.

"What are you looking at?"

"Your feet, girl. Is there anything about you that I'm not going like?" He was smiling as he tried to hand her the blunt.

"I don't smoke," she said, as she leaned against him in the doorway.

"So you came over here because it was killing you to be that far away from me?"

"Whatever. Don't flatter yourself." She tried to push away, but he wrapped his arms around her waist and pulled her right up against him.

She looked up at him and licked her lips nervously. Then before she knew what was happing, he leaned in and pressed his lips against hers. Their mouths opened. His tongue slid inside her mouth and met hers. They began to kiss. Her lips were softer than what he imagined. There was so much passion between them that he could feel himself rising and had to pull away. She held onto him and laid her head on his chest for a while. Then he put the blunt back and they walked to the couch with their drinks and sat down.

He was about to kiss her again when the house phone rang. He got up and picked the phone up off the dining room table. He put it on speaker as he sat back down.

"Hello?" It was the guard at the front gates.

"Mr. Mack, there's someone by the name of Blazz who's here to see you."

"Yes, you can let him in."

"Ok, sir."

Kat was laughing.

"What's so funny?" He frowned.

"Nothing, I'm sorry. It's just that…" She was still laughing, trying to get it all out. "You have that man calling you by your nickname. That's ghetto, Travon."

He smiled, seeing her mistake. "That's my name."

She stopped laughing and stared at him to see if he was serious. "Are you for real? That's really your name?"

"Yes. Travon Williams Mack."

"Oh, I thought T-Mack was like a little hood name or something. I'm sorry, babe."

Babe. He liked the way that sounded coming out her mouth. He leaned in and kissed her again. She wrapped her arms around his neck. She felt so good next to him. He could see himself laying up with her all day.

Then they were interrupted by the doorbell. He tried to stand up, but she held onto him.

"I have to answer the door, ma. It's my little brother."

"Ohhh, ok." He kissed her on the forehead as he got back up.

The doorbell rang again. "I'm coming. Hold up, nigga."

He unlocked the door and let his little brother in. "What up, little bro?"

"What up, dawg. What took you so long?" he was saying as he walked through the door.

Then he spotted Kat on the couch watching TV.

"Oh I see, it's like that, huh?" Blazz was grinning and tried to give his brother some dap, but Mack just ignored him.

"Nigga, just lock my door and mind your business."

"Man, whatever. Just fire that shit up. I ain't smoked all day," Blazz was saying as he sat down on the couch across from Kat and Mack.

"Kat, this my no-manner-having ass little brother Blazz. Bro this is my friend, Kat. Speak next time before you start begging for shit," he told him as he gave him the blunt and ashtray. "You know the rules. No smoking in the spot, so take that shit outside."

"Yeah, yeah, I know. But first off, I was not begging for shit, and second off I was about to speak if you gave me a chance."

"Whatever, nigga. You had your chance when you walked through the door, blood."

Kat was enjoying the two brothers interact. She was seeing a different side of Mack. She wished that her and her brother got along like that. You could tell they loved each other. Even though they were talking shit, she knew that was a guy thing.

"So you guys got a new coach this year? You better hope he let you get away with missing all those practices, nigga. Most coaches will just bench your ass."

"Don't worry about me, bro. When you play like me, you can do what the fuck you want and still play every game."

Mack just shook his head. He wished that Blazz would just listen sometimes instead of always having something smart to say. He didn't want him to throw his talent away. Blazz was good, but his attitude sucked and talent can only get you so far. The streets and prisons were full of talented people.

"You keep thinking that way little bro and we'll see how far it gets you."

Blazz was tired of the pep talk. He came by to get some money from Mack, not hear he was fucking up. He got enough of that from his mom at home.

"Yeah I hear you, but I need to get home. So can you shoot me that dough and drop me off at the house?"

Mack was glaring at his brother. He knew that he was not listening to him. He was tired of his attitude. He didn't want to see him fuck his life up, but he didn't know how to get through to him. The only reason he gave him money was so he didn't have to go out in the streets and hustle. Blazz knew what Mack did and would always ask to go with him, but Mack was not having that. He wanted Blazz to stay in school and stay out of trouble, but it seemed the older Blazz got, the wilder he was getting. He would just have to stay on him.

Mack was about to get up when he noticed Kat had fallen asleep. He tried to wake her up, but she was out cold. He picked her up and carried her to the bedroom, laid her down and pulled the covers over her. He went to his walk-in closet and opened the door. It was filled with clothes and pants along one side, shirts in the middle and jackets and hoodies on the other side. The top shelf and the floor were filled with shoeboxes. He walked to the back, kneeled down and moved a row of shoeboxes, exposing a black safe with a keypad. He punched the combination in. It beeped three times then popped open. He reached in and pulled out a brown paper bag full of money, opened it up, took five thousand out and one of his guns. He then closed the safe back up. He got up and grabbed his Louie duffel bag off the top shelf and dumped the rest of the money from the paper bag in it. He threw the bag over his shoulder, put his gun in the waistband of his jeans, and then pulled his shirt over it.

As he walked out of the room, he stopped and looked at Kat. She looked beautiful sleeping in his king size bed. He wished he could stay and lay with her, but he had to take his brother home and drop the money off. He turned the lights off and closed the door.

T-Mack and Blazz got off the Freeway at Century and headed east. Rundown homes, liquor stores and gas stations were the scenery. There was plenty of traffic, even though it was ten at night. They stopped at a red light. A cop car sped by with its lights and sirens on. The light turned green. T-Mack began to pull off.

"Here, little nigga." He tossed a roll of hundreds in Blazz's lap. "When school start back, just try to stay focused, man. That's all I'm asking you to do so you can get up off this Eastside and be somebody."

"I know, Mack, but shit. It's hard. My mom be tripping. She want a nigga in the house at ten o'clock and shit. A nigga sixteen."

"Hard, nigga? You don't know what hard is. I give yo ass five hundred a week and you done wrecked three wipes I bought yo ass. You spoiled, nigga. That's your problem."

Blazz just sat there staring out the window. He hated when Mack talked to him like a kid. He couldn't wait for him to realize he was a man now and give him some work so he could make some real money. He would have to make him realize he was not a little boy anymore.

CHAPTER 7

On 82nd and Hooper across the street from Blazz's house, Blue, M-Rock, and Chase sat on the front porch drinking cognac.

"Chase, when you gonna put a nigga on, cause a nigga fresh out. Hook a nigga up."

M-rock had just got out of prison two weeks ago and was broke. Even though Chase gave him $1500 when he got out, he had spent it all on weed, alcohol, and women. Now he was looking for another handout. Mostly everyone in the hood was terrified of him because he was known to be a killer. He once gunned a man down in a dice game over $40, but Chase was a OG from eight five Gangsta Crip. All three men on the block were members, but Chase was their big homie. He was a 36-year-old drug dealer and everyone in their hood respected him.

"Check this out, cuzz. I just gave you some bread last week. You must think you my bitch or something. What the fuck, you trick that shit off?"

"Naw, cuz. You know how it is. I had bills and shit, that's all. You a baller, cuzz. Why you acting like that?"

"Nigga, what bills you got, cuzz? You just got out!" They all started laughing.

"Pass that bottle, cuzz," Blue said as he held out his hand.

"Hold on, cuzz. You thrust ass nigga, you act like yo young ass ain't had no yak before. It ain't going nowhere."

Blue was 18, five years younger than M-Rock, but stood six feet tall, weighing 200 pounds. He was much bigger than M-Rock who stood 5'8" and was 160 pounds. So M-Rock always gave him a hard time, letting Blue know who was boss.

"Cuzz, you always tripping."

"Damn right, nigga. You thought…" M-Rock paused for a second and stared at a car that had parked across the street from them.

"Cuzz, who the fuck is that,?" The other two men stopped what they were doing and looked at the black Benz parked across the street.

"Oh, that's that nigga Blazz and his brother T-Mack," Blue said as he got the bottle.

"Y'all still ain't put that nigga Blazz on the hood, cuzz? What's up with that? And look at that nigga brother pulling up like he from over here. I don't like that shit, cuzz. You see that piece around his neck?"

"Yeah, cuz. That nigga Blazz told me that chain his brother got around his neck cost like thirty G's, cuzz."

"Blue, you telling me you let that nigga come to the hood with a thirty thousand dollar chain and leave with that shit, as broke as you is, cuzz? You should get dp'ed for that shit."

"What the fuck you want me to do?"

M-Rock looked at Blue and shook his head. He knew Blue was young, but you just don't let a nigga come through shining like that. He knew Chase was not tripping because he already had paper, but M-Rock was starving and he couldn't sit back and let this nigga get off the block with that chain.

"I'ma show you what to do, cuzz. Come on."

M-Rock stood up and went to the bushes and grabbed his 44 magnum. He was about to walk across the street when Chase stopped him.

"Hold on, cuzz. You can't do that shit right here. You gonna make the spot hot, nigga. Use your head, cuzz."

"Man, we got to get that nigga, cuzz. Fuck the spot. I'm broke, cuzz."

"Nigga, I ain't telling you not to get him, just don't do that shit here. Follow that nigga, cuzz. Use your fucking head. If you get that nigga right here, Blazz's mom Miss Jackson is definitely gonna call the law. She probably looking out the window right now."

"Yeah, you right, Blue. Soon as cuzz pull off, we gonna hop in my ride and follow him."

Blue took another drink and shook his head yes. "I'm with it, loc."

Chase had a bad feeling about this, but knew there was no talking M-Rock out of it. Chase never fucked with T-Mack because Mack's reputation was well known and if M-Rock would stay out of jail long enough to see what was going down on the street, he would know that T-Mack was crazy and was not to be fucked with.

"Blue, run in the house and grab the MAC 11 out the stash," Chase told him as he stood up on the porch.

Blue went in the house and walked back out with the gun wrapped in a towel.

"Make sure that nigga don't see y'all following him, cuzz, and don't hesitate to bust on his ass if he try anything."

"You ain't got to tell me, cuzz. This is what I do, nigga. He ain't even gonna see it coming."

M-Rock couldn't wait. He already knew what he was going to do with the chain once he got it. He would have Chase take it to his connect and get as much dope as he could get for it, then it would be his time to shine.

Mack drove off once Blazz had made it in the house safely. He called Kat's cell phone to see if she had woken up, but got no answer. He had to make one more stop before he headed home to her. He crossed down Central Blvd. headed downtown. It was getting late and there were fewer cars on the street now. He crossed Slauson ave and was now driving through the 50's, the heart of his hood. There were a few of his homies out on the Blvd. doing their thing. Some threw their hands up, flashing gang signs at him and the car behind him.

A few minutes later his phone rang. He picked it up thinking it was Kat. He had been thinking about her since he had left the house. He checked the caller ID. It was his homie sane, an older homie that was always on the block slanging and banging.

"What up, my nigga."

"Shit, just out on the Ave. Blood, where you headed? I seen you roll by."

"You know me, blood. Out taking care of business. What up though?"

"There was a car behind you with two niggas in it, a dark brown Caprice. The homies banged on it and the passenger threw up 85 Gangsta Crip. I was about to bust on they ass, but one time hit the corner."

"They probably just headed to the 43's. I think I see them right now. I'm ah keep my eyes on them. Good looking."

"Alright, blood."

"Alright, later."

He hung up the phone and got the hk 9mm out of the stash. He was leaving the 40's and headed through the 30's now. It was all blood territory now until you got to downtown, but the brown Caprice was still behind him. He made a left when he got to 27th street. Usually this street was full of niggas. It was headquarters for the 20 outlaw bloods, but tonight it was deserted. He saw a car turn on the same street as him. He couldn't tell if it was the same brown Caprice, so he pulled into a random driveway and waited. Then the car passed him by and it was a brown Caprice, the same brown Caprice that was parked on 85th in front of his brother's house. The niggas had been following him since he left from over there.

"What the fuck do they want?" he thought.

He knew they did not know about the money. He hadn't even told Blazz what was in the bag. He reached back in his stash spot and pulled out two more clips. He did know what they wanted, but he knew what they would get if they tried anything.

He backed out the driveway and drove back to Central and made a left, heading downtown. He still needed to drop the money off before shit got hectic. He was driving a little fast now, trying to make every light. He crossed over Washington Blvd. He was almost there now. He made a quick right, then a left and pulled to the front gate of a ten-story 24-hour storage facility where he rented two storage places in two different names.

He entered the code for the storage space in his name. The gate went up and he pulled in fast, parked, grabbed his bag and his gun, then jumped out and looked around. He was in the underground parking area. There was only one other car there; a black Lexus that looked like it had parked there for years.

He headed for the elevator. He was safe for now. If the brown car was still following him, there was no way the drivers could get in there without a storage code for the gate. Mack had two storage units there because if the cops ever found out about this place and came in asking questions about him, the manager would think he had the one storage that was in his name. When he went down there, he only used that code to enter the facility. The other storage unit was rented online by a Juan Martinez and he paid the rent every month online with a prepaid credit card with the same name, so there was no way of knowing he had two storage spaces there.

He got off the elevator on the ninth floor where both spaces were located and walked to 912 and unlocked the lock. He walked in, and then turned the light on. He hadn't been there in two weeks, but everything looked the same. The space was filled with black trash bags full of clothes he bought from a secondhand store. He sat his duffle bag down and began moving bags out the way. When he was done, he was standing in front of a five-foot tall gray fireproof safe. It weighed eight hundred pounds and had a hydraulic locking system that was controlled by an electronic keypad. He put the code in and pushed enter. He could hear the locks moving. Then it beeped five times.

His phone began to ring, but he did not check to see who it was. The safe alerted him that it had been opened. He looked in the safe and it was all there: rows and rows of money. $750,000. Once he put the money from his bag in, he would have close to $900,000.

It was time for him to take a break. With the four murders that had just happened, he needed to lay low for a while and take it easy. He finished putting the money from the bag in and closed the safe. He waited a second for it to lock, and then he left.

He drove out of the parking lot and looked up the street both ways, then turned right and headed for the freeway. Behind him up the street, the brown Caprice turned its lights on and pulled away from the curb in pursuit.

Kat opened her eyes and looked around. At first she didn't realize where she was, but then she sat up in the king size bed and it started to come back to her. She remembered going out to eat and all the wine she had been drinking then and how Travon came back to his house to meet his brother. She was trying hard to remember everything that happened after that.

"Why am I in his bed? Did we have sex? Oh shit, I hope I didn't sleep with him. It's way too soon. He gonna think I'm a ho."

She jumped up out the bed and turned the light on. There were three doors in the room. One was open and she could see that it was the bathroom. She walked in and closed the door. The marble floor was cold on her bare feet. She unbuckled her belt and pulled down her pants, then sat down on the toilet and began to pee. Then it hit her. She still had all her clothes on, plus she didn't feel like she had sex and it had been a long time since she had been with anyone, so she would definitely feel something. She was relieved she hadn't done anything to make Travon think she was easy. She really liked him. She hadn't felt this way in a while -- maybe never had -- and she didn't want to do anything to mess it up.

Her head was spinning. She was still a little tipsy. She got up, flushed the toilet and washed her hands. She splashed some water on her face, turned to leave, then stopped, turned back around and opened the medicine cabinet. Then she knelt down and opened the doors under the sink. She smiled to herself. There was not one trace of a woman.

She walked through the bedroom and opened the door leading into the living room. The house was quiet. She called out Travon's name, but there was no answer. All the lights were on. She saw her purse on the couch and her phone on the coffee table. She picked the phone up. It was dead.

"Shit."

She wondered how many calls she missed. As she got her charger out and looked for an outlet, she found one on the side of the couch. She plugged the phone up to charge, went to the kitchen and got some water to drink out of the fridge. Then she went back and sat down on the couch. She wondered where Travon had gone. She was a little upset that he left her all alone, but she figured he probably had a good reason. He probably had some business to take care of. She already figured that he wasn't a boxer. He probably sold drugs like Sunshine said. She thought his car and his condo were way too fly. He was always meeting with his cousin, and when he came out his cousin's house, that Louie backpack was empty. She might be young, but she knew a hustler when she saw one. She reached for her phone and powered it on, then checked her messages. Sunshine had left six, her mom left one and a few of her friends from school, but nothing from Travon. She was a little disappointed that he hadn't called and she hoped he wasn't out with another girl. If he was, she would have to cut him off, she told herself.

"You just don't leave someone at your house to go fuck with someone else and think you can come back and be with me," she thought.

She looked his number up, and then pushed the call button. It began to ring. She smiled. He hadn't turned his phone off. That was a good sign. It rang three more times and his answering service picked up.

"Shit."

She hung up. She wasn't ready to leave a message yet. She would just call back and if he didn't answer that time, then she would leave him a message and let him know she was not one to be treated like this.

"You just don't leave a person in your house and disappear, then not answer your phone," she fumed.

Maybe the other girls he fucked with put up with it, but she didn't have to. Then her phone rang, interrupting her thoughts. She checked the caller ID. It was him. She pressed talk and put the phone to her ear.

"Hello," she said with an attitude.

"Hey ma, what's wrong? You sound upset. I hope you not mad at me for leaving you at my house, but I had to take my brother home and you were knocked out. I tried to wake you, but it was no use, so I put you in my bed. But I'm on my way back now."

She was relieved he had a good reason for leaving. She felt bad for thinking he was out with another girl.

"No, I'm not mad. I just woke up right before you called. I Haden even notice you left," she lied to him.

She couldn't tell him the truth. She would look stupid. Plus if he knew how jealous she had been feeling, it might scare him away.

"Well, I will be there soon, ok ma?"

"Ok, T."

She hung up. She couldn't help but feel better knowing he would be there soon.

She picked the remote up, turned the flat screen on and flipped through the channels. Then her phone rang. She looked at the caller ID. It was Sunshine.

"Hello?"

"Bitch, what the fuck you been doing? I been calling yo young ass for hours and you ain't even call a bitch back!" she yelled through the phone, her voice trying to compete with the loud rap song in the background.

"I can barely hear you, girl. Where you at? The club?"

"Yeah, hold on."

A few seconds later, you could hear a door close and it got much quieter. Even though you could hear girls talking to one another, you could barely hear the music now.

"I was at the bar. I had to come in the dressing room. Bitch, it's cracking up in here tonight. You need to get your yellow ass up here. Where the fuck you been? I been calling you all day."

"I'm still with T. We been together all day. I'm at his condo right now."

Kat was trying her hardest to sound as if it was nothing to her. She didn't want Sunshine to know how excited she was and the feeling she was beginning to feel for T-Mack, because Sunshine had a way of making her feel like a child.

"Where that nigga stay, girl? Is his house as fly as his wipe?" You could tell that Sunshine was excited and wanted to know more by how fast she was talking.

"He stay in Westchester in these condos by Friday's. It's cool. It got waterfalls in the front and a park in the middle and his condo has white carpet, a big ass fish tank and a fireplace. It's cool."

"Damn, bitch. That shit sound fly. You hit the jackpot, but you need to get up here and get some of this money. I already made five hundred, bitch."

"I'm waiting for him to come back from dropping his little brother off at his mom's house, then I'll come through."

"You telling me that nigga left you in his house by yourself? That nigga must really be feeling you. If I was you, I would be going through all that nigga shit seeing what I could come up on. He might have a safe in that bitch."

Sunshine was from the hood and already set up a few ballers for her homies to rob, but Kat had never done anything like that even though when she was a child she had it rough. She had been raised by middle class parents and was brought up with values. She wouldn't dream of setting up anyone, let alone T-Mack. Not with the way she felt about him.

"Yeah, I know you would, but I don't get down like that. I'll call you when I'm on my way to the club."

"Ok girl. You better hurry up while the money still here."

"Alright, bye."

Kat had no intention of going to the club, but she didn't want to let Sunshine know because she would have asked a thousand questions. She didn't need her all in her business, but all she planned on doing was staying with T-Mack for as long as she could.

CHAPTER 8

T-Mack had spotted the brown Caprice a little while after he got on the freeway. He had made several maneuvers to be sure he was being followed. Now that he was sure, he had to plan his next move. He picked the blunt up out of the ashtray and lit it, then reached up and pushed the button to open the sunroof. As he hit the blunt and listened to an old Biggie song "Niggas bleed just like us", his plan came together.

M-rock and Blue had been following T-Mack for a while now and they both were getting restless. They were ready to make a move as soon as the opportunity presented itself.

"Man, cuzz. This nigga making me mad, dawg. When his bitch ass gone stop so we can get his ass and go get some more yack?"

He threw the empty bottle out the window. Blue was disappointed as he saw the last of the liquor go down M-Rock's throat and the empty bottle go out the window, but he knew better than to complain, so he took his frustration out on Mack.

"Cuzz, this nigga gone make me kill his ass whenever he pull over. Got a nigga on a wild goose chase and shit. Where the fuck we going?" Blue was saying as he gripped the MAC-11 submachine gun tightly in his hand, ready to use it.

Normally he would be scared because he was not the robbing and killing type like M-Rock, but the alcohol had his mind in a haze and he felt like he was invincible.

"Hold up, cuzz. He changing lanes." M-Rock paused for a minute.

"Yeah, he getting off. Get ready…damn, this nigga driving fast, cuzz."

The Benz made a quick right turn as it exited the freeway, then went down two blocks and made another quick right, then a left onto a residential street with lots of cars parked on both sides. M-Rock turned the corner a few seconds later and saw the Benz double-parked up the block.

"There he go cuzz. You ready?" he said as he pulled the Caprice right behind the S55 Benz.

"You think he in there? I can't see shit behind that limo tint, cuzz," Blue was saying as he took the safety off the MAC-11.

"You think he gone leave a hundred thousand dollar car on rims in the middle of the street in this raggedy ass hood so some crack head can jump in and drive off?" M-Rock looked at Blue like he was the dumbest nigga on the Eastside. "Let's go, stupid."

As Blue reached for the door, he felt something cold on the side of his temple and before he could look up to see what or who it was, the inside of the car lit up bright white like a flash from a camera had went off inside. The lights went off in his young eyes as his brains went flying out the other side of his skull and into M-Rock's lap. His lifeless corpse slumped in the passenger seat.

M-Rock was totally caught off guard. His first instinct was to smash off, but in a panic, he forgot about the Benz in front of him and smashed right into it. The back window of the car shattered as bullets from T-Mack's 40 Glock tore through it. M-Rock ducked down below the steering wheel of the big old car and returned fire wildly.

BAM BAM BAM BAM BAM!

He unloaded the 44 magnum, praying that he hit something. It was quiet for a split second. Then the bullets began to rain down on him, hitting everything around him.

"How many fucking clips this nigga got?" he thought.

Then a bullet tore into his shoulder and he knew he had to do something or he was going to die right next to his boy Blue. That's when he saw the MAC-11 with the 50-round clip in Blue's lap. He pulled it out of Blue's hands, and then threw the car in reverse while bullets were zinging by his head, barely missing their mark. He pushed the gas pedal to the floor and aimed the MAC-11 out the window.

At the same time, fire lit up the night as the fully automatic unloaded all 50 rounds in less than 3 seconds. T-Mack dove back behind the white Astro van he had been hiding behind when M-Rock had pulled up and hit the ground. Bullets smashed through the side of the van and three cars behind it.

"What the fuck? That nigga busting with some Iraqi shit!" T-Mack thought as he turned over on his back to look and make sure the nigga wasn't coming back.

He got up off the ground just in time to see the brown car burn rubber as it turned the corner. He looked around and saw that porch lights were coming on and people were beginning to look out their windows. He ran to his car, jumped in and sped off. He put the Glock and the 30-round extended clip back in the stash, then checked his body to make sure he wasn't hit. As soon as he was far enough out of the area, he pulled over onto a side street and parked. Then he pulled out his cell phone and called Solo.

"What up, dawg? Where you at?" he yelled in the phone as he looked around the neighborhood he was in, his adrenaline still pumping from the shootout.

"I'm at the house in the 90's. What's up? You sound out of breath, blood. What the fuck up with you?" Solo asked as he pushed a stripper's head back down in his lap.

"Check this out, nigga. I'm about 10 minutes from your house. Put this address in your navigation and get over here ASAP. This shit is serious. I'll fill you in when you get here."

"Ok, blood. Say no more. What's the address?" Solo said, pushing the girl off him as he jumped up to get dressed.

T-Mack looked around until he saw a number in white on the curb and gave it to Solo with the street name. "Hurry up, nigga."

"I'm on my way right now," Solo yelled over his shoulder as he went out the front door. "I'll be right back, baby. Make yourself at home."

Ten minutes later, Solo turned the corner and spotted T-Mack's black Benz. He parked his Challenger across the street from Mack and got out and walked across to him. As he approached the car, he noticed the damage to the back.

"Damn, blood. What the fuck happened to you, nigga? You wrecked the S55 blood? You tripping, dawg?" Solo said as he inspected the damage to the trunk and back bumper.

"Man, you ain't gone believe what happen. But what took you so long, nigga?" Mack said as he got out of the car and hit the alarm.

"Nigga, ain't no nigga gonna steal that shit looking like that, dawg," Solo said, laughing as Mack got in the car.

"Fuck you, blood." Mack was not in a playful mood.

"Alright, nigga. So what happened? I know this shit got to be good," Solo said as he pulled off.

He was burning rubber as he hit the gas a little too hard, trying to hurry up and drop T-Mack off so he could get back to the girl.

Chapter 9

Twenty minutes later, T-Mack walked through the front door of his condo talking on the phone with his little bro.

"The nigga Solo on his way to pick you up and take you to get a room. Grab everything you need and be ready when he pull up."

"What the fuck you talking about, T? You tripping, nigga? You high or something?" Blazz said as he sat up in bed and put his X-box on pause.

He had been playing Call of Duty online against some New York niggas and was about to take one of them out.

"Listen, some shit just jumped off and you ain't safe over there, so get yo shit together and be ready when Solo pull up and that's all you need to know."

Mack was getting hot. He was not in the mood for a debate, but Blazz never made anything easy.

"I'm in the middle..."

T-Mack cut him off in mid-sentence.

"Shut the fuck up and have yo black ass ready when Solo get there, nigga," he yelled as he hung up the phone and walked into the living room were Kat had been sleeping on the couch until his voice woke her up.

She smiled at him as she sat up on the couch. "What time is it, T?"

He sat down next to her and couldn't help but notice how beautiful she was. His feeling for her had been growing stronger day by day since he meet her and he knew that if he didn't catch himself, he could easily fall in love, a thing he knew little about. Up to this point, he only loved his brother and his mother, and his mother had died three years ago of lung cancer while he was locked down in CYA. He was the only child and they loved each other dearly and he still had not gotten over the fact that he was not there for her last days.

"Oh, it's 11:30, ma," he said looking at his Rolex.

He picked up the remote, turned from the info commercials that were on and went to his TIVO library. He selected one of his favorite movies, "Heat", and pressed play.

"I had a little car accident so…"

Kat turned to him with a look of shock and concern on her face. "Are you alright, babe? Did you get hurt?"

She looked him up and down to make sure he was ok.

"Yeah, ma. Don't trip. I'm alright. Calm down, babe," he said as he wrapped his arms around her.

She hugged him back, holding onto him tight. "What happened? Did anyone get hurt?"

He could tell she was genuinely concerned and for some reason, it made him feel good that someone cared and about him.

"No, babe. No one got hurt. I was at a stop sign and some drunk Mexican ran into the back of my shit. When I pulled over, the nigga kept going. My shit is fucked up."

"Did you get that mutha fucka's license plate, babe? Those mutha fuckas always doing that shit. They hit my mom's car last year."

T-Mack was surprised to hear Kat talk like that. She had a little gangsteri-sahm about her and he liked how she had his back.

"Wow, little mama. I know that ain't the same mouth you kissed me with earlier," he said, laughing as he pulled back so he could see her face.

"Whatever," she said, blushing as she buried her head back in his chest.

"I was saying though, whenever you ready to go, I can call you a cab. I know it's late though, so if you want, you can spend the night here and in the morning you can help me pick out a new car. Then I'll take you home."

"I don't know, T."

He knew what she was thinking, so he quickly cut her off.

"It ain't even like that, ma. I would never get at you like that," he said, as he looked her in the eyes. "I just thought we could kick it, you know, watch movies until we fall asleep on the sofa, that's all. I'm really feeling you and I'm just not ready for you to go."

The look on his face was so sincere, she had to look away She felt that he needed her and she needed him and she wasn't ready to leave either, so she looked back into his eyes and said one soft word.

"Ok."

Then she buried her head back in his chest. He pulled her closer as she lay there in his arms. She felt safer than she had ever felt before.

᛭

T-Mack and Kat walked into the GM dealership on Figueroa by USC. On the showroom floor was the new Camaro, DTS, CTS-V Coupe, a Vet and a fully loaded black on black Escalade on 22" Cadillac rims. T-Mack's mind was already made up that fast. He knew he would be leaving in that truck, but he still wanted to see what Kat's taste was.

"What can you picture me rolling in, ma?" he said, following behind her as she strolled from car to car.

"That one looks like something my grandma would drive," she said, frowning and pointing to the DTS.

"And those two look like something I would drive," she said, smiling and pointing at the CTS-V Coupe and Vet.

"You like those, huh?" Mack was saying as he looked inside one of the small cars.

He couldn't see himself in either one.

"Yeah I like them, but not for you, babe. I think you would look good in this truck," she said as she opened up the passenger side door.

She liked how roomie it was. T-Mack climbed in the driver's side and closed the door so he could get a feel for it. The inside had black leather wood grain, navigation, OnStar, a sunroof, dropped down TVs in the back, Bluetooth, satellite radio and much more. The truck was loaded and he loved it.

"I think you're wrong, ma," Mack said as he turned and smiled at her. "*We* gone look good in this truck."

She climbed in the truck and was about to respond to him when an elderly white man approached them.

"How's it going?" he said with a big smile.

The man looked at Mack and Kat, trying to determine if they could afford the truck they were in. Then he noticed the presidential Rolex T-Mack had on, a watch he had wanted for years and that answered his question. The young black guy could definitely afford the truck.

"I see you have good taste, sir. This truck is the best luxury truck there is and..."

Mack cut the sales man off before he could even start his sales pitch. "We'll take it."

The man looked a little confused. He had never sold a car that fast before. They didn't even ask the price. He was already calculating his commission. He hoped this guy was serious and had damn good credit or a big down payment.

"Yes, sir. Now let's get you over to my computer so we can run your credit. What's your score like?" he said as he led T-Mack and Kat to his office.

"I will be paying cash."

The man stopped dead in his tracks. He turned around and looked Mack in his face to see if he was serious. Once he realized he was, he rushed them into his office and got the head manager. They both returned quickly with big smiles on their faces.

"The truck is roughly eighty thousand. It's a special edition. They only made a hundred of them. Do you have the cash on you right now?" the head manager asked nervously.

T-Mack picked up the backpack full of money he had Solo bring him that morning and dumped it on the table.

"I got to be somewhere in a hour, so make it fast," Mack said.

He looked at his watch impatiently while Kat just stared in amazement. She definitely knew he was not a boxer and she wanted to ask him what he did to have so much money, but she felt she had no right because she too had not told him about her late night activities. At this point it really didn't matter, however. She had already made up her mind that this was the man she wanted to spend every day of her life with. She had fallen for him fast and hard and she hoped he felt the same way too.

Chapter 10

Blazz passed the blunt back to Bo as they watched the traffic go by on Adams Blvd. Blazz had been waiting on T-Mack to come by and pick him up.

"Where the fuck this nigga at, dawg? It's going on eight o'clock. He was supposed to be here at two," Blazz said as he got the blunt back.

"Man, this some good shit, blood. This Mack shit?" Bo asked as he struggled not to cough from the potent smoke.

"Yeah, that nigga got a cool connect up north. You know how my bro do."

"I need like a pound of this shit," Bo said as he got up off the porch and walked to the gate to meet a customer.

"What you need, my nigga?"

"Shit man, a zip, that's all," said Black, a young nigga from Neighborhood 20 bloods, the same hood that Bo was from.

Bo was a 23-year-old hustler from the Westside. Him and Mack went to elementary and junior high together and were good friends over the years. They had put in a lot of work together and had grown to trust each other. He was well respected as a high-ranking member of his hood.

"Seven-fifty, nigga."

"Seven-fifty, shit. I got like seven-twenty-five," Black said, counting his money as Bo let him through the gate.

"Blood, yo ass is always short, nigga. This the last time on 20's. You gone be fucked up when you got to go fuck with killa. That nigga gone charge you eight-hundred and his shit can't fuck with mine," Bo replied as he took the money and recounted it.

He walked in the house and came back out and handed Black a plastic sandwich bag full of crack cocaine.

"Alight, blood. I holla back tonight or in the morning," Black said as he walked out the gate.

"The nigga think he slick, always coming short, but what his dumb ass don't know when he short me, I short him, so the only thing not short in the deal is the money," Bo said smiling.

He knew every dollar counted in the game and he was trying to win, not lose.

"I'm about to call this nigga. I bet he don't even answer," Blazz said as he got his cell phone out to call T-Mack.

Just as he was dialing the number, a brand new Escalade on 26" black rims with a silver lip pulled up with bass so loud it shook the porch.

"Who the fuck is that?" Bo said as he grabbed his 9mm from under the chair he was sitting on.

"Fuck if I know, nigga. This yo hood, not mine," Blazz said as he prepared for anything that might happen.

Then the tinted window rolled down and they saw T-Mack.

"What up, blood. Come on, nigga," he called to Blazz as he turned the music down.

Both men got up off the porch, happy to see T-Mack. Blazz got in on the passenger side and Bo stopped at the window.

"What up, blood. This how you doing it, huh? Goddamn, this shit is hard," Bo said as he checked out the truck.

"Yeah, I just snatched it up two weeks ago. It's been at 310 getting hooked up. I had to slip that nigga extra to put me in front, otherwise my shit would have been there for months."

"Shit, I guess you got it like that. It must be nice. But check this out, I need you to hit me with one of those p's of that 0.6 kush."

"Blazz little ass put you up on game, huh? That shit is some fire straight from Humboldt, nigga," T-Mack said as he punched in a number on his cell phone.

The bottom part of the back seat popped up like a trunk and he reached back and pulled out a pound of kush weed sealed in an airtight bag and placed it on Blazz's lap. Blazz and Bo both stared at T-Mack as if he just pulled a rabbit out of his ass.

"I thought you just bought this shit, nigga. How the fuck you get that stash put in that fast, bro?"

Mack just smiled.

"Like I said, I had to pay my boy extra. Money talks and you know the rest," he said as he leaned back in his seat. "But fuck all that, let's get back to business. That OG going for forty-four, but you can give me thirty-six hundred. You know you my boy."

"That's what I'm talking about," Bo said as he pulled out a wad of cash, counted out thirty-six hundred and tossed it to T-Mack.

Then he grabbed the pound and tucked it under his shirt.

"Alright blood, be safe," Bo yelled as he quickly walked back in the yard and locked the gate.

Mack pulled off as he tossed the roll of cash in the stash without counting it.

"Man, where the fuck you been, nigga?" Blazz said as he rolled up his window.

"I been laying low, nigga. Too much shit been jumping off in the last few weeks. I had to make sure I wasn't hot, blood," Mack said as he turned the corner onto Crenshaw Blvd.

He passed by a group of girls at the bus stop waiving at his truck. He sped by without noticing them.

"Yeah, Solo told me what happened nigga and guess what?" Blazz asked without waiting for an answer.

"The nigga M-Rock made it to the hospital and passed out in the parking lot and when he woke up, he was handcuffed to the bed. His parole officer violated his ass for getting shot, can you believe that shit?" Blazz said laughing.

Mack was thinking about what happened that night. The only regret he had was that he didn't get to finish M-Rock off. If he ever ran across the nigga again, he wouldn't be so lucky, he thought.

"And the nigga told his people that he know who did the shit and when he get out he gone kill the nigga." Blazz was looking at his brother to see how he took the news, but Mack remained expressionless for a moment.

Then he started busting up laughing. He was laughing so hard his eyes started to water.

"Man, those broke ass niggas better get their money up, way up, before they even think about stepping to me and my niggas. I'll take the niggas whole hood in one week. They only got one little ass block. Fuck those niggas. You just gotta keep yo ass from over there and let me worry about them," he said as he wiped his eyes.

He pulled in the alley and stopped in front of the black metal gate that was about ten feet high. He hit a gate opener and it began to slide open. As T-Mack pulled the truck in, a motion-activated light came on, lighting up the back parking lot. T-Mack opened up the back door to a two-story building and they entered into a small, office-like room.

"This my new spot. I'm make it a barbershop," he said as he showed Blazz around. "The front is big, but ain't shit in there right now. But I'm put like ten barber stations up there and on the other side I'ma have shit for sale like hats, t-shirts, shoes and shit like that. But check this out."

T-Mack walked to another bar door and opened it up. There were stairs leading up to a top floor. When they reached the top, they walked through another bar door and walked into a big open room. To the right there was a nice sized kitchen with granite counter tops and stainless steel appliances. Straight ahead there was a pool table and a full bar behind that, both stainless steel, even the bar stools. To the left were dark red leather couches and the walls were dark red with white crown molding. On one wall was a red, sixty-inch flat screen. The hardwood floors were a cherry wood and there were big abstract paintings on all the walls with different shades of reds, browns and other earth tones.

"Man, this shit is tight," Blazz said looking around, wondering how much T-Mack had spent putting this place together.

"You ain't seen the best part," T-Mack said as he opened up the door on the other side of the room.

They walked through the door into a big bedroom with a king size bed. The floor was covered with thick brown shag carpeting. The walls were cream with brown molding. There were African style paintings on three of the walls. The wall in front of them had vertical blinds that went from celling to floor and from wall to wall. T-Mack hit a switch on the wall and the blinds began to slowly part in the middle, revealing a wall made of glass from top to bottom. Blazz walked to the wall and looked out. He could see cars driving up and down Crenshaw Blvd.

"Man, this shit is crazy, bro. Damn, look at those bitches in the Beamer," Blazz said as he waved, trying to get the girls' attention.

"Nigga, they can't see yo dumb ass. This shit is like a one-way mirror. You think I'm have people looking all up in my bedroom, crazy?" Mack said as he lay on the bed.

He answered his phone. "What up, nigga? What's good?"

He took an ounce of kush out of his pocket and threw it at Blazz.

"The blunts is on the bar, bro," he said, putting the phone back to his ear.

"What up, nigga. I'm in the back. Buzz me in." It was his cousin Solo.

He had not seen him since he dropped the money off for the Escalade two weeks ago. He pressed power on the remote that was lying on the bed and the painting on the left wall slid down, revealing a fifty-inch flat screen. He turned to channel three and the screen split into six sections, showing surveillance footage of angles and part of the shop. He could see Solo's Challenger in the back alley on the other side of the gate.

"Yeah, I see you. Come on," he said as he hit a button on the control panel by the light switch.

The gate began to open. Solo walked through the upstairs door with a big bottle of Patron in one hand and a bottle of Nuvo in the other. Behind him were four beautiful woman.

"This the Cherry Lounge ladies. What happens here stays here, so feel free to let yourself go and get loose," Solo said, laughing.

The women started laughing with him as they sat down in the living room. Blazz was still rolling blunts at the bar. He stopped momentarily to check out the females. The black one was light-skinned with long, curly hair that went to the middle of her back. She was about 5'8" with a very nice shape. She weighed about 120 with hazel eyes. Two of the girls were obviously twins. They were tall, about 5'10", and were slim with straight black hair that fell to their shoulders. They had caramel complexions and Asian-like eyes with full lips. They could have easily passed for runway models. The other one was a Spanish girl. She had long, honey-blond hair with copper tone highlights. She was the shortest of them, coming in at 5'2". Her breasts were small, but her hips and butt would make J Lo look bad. Blazz could tell they were at least his brother's age or older and the way they were dressed in Louie, Gucci, Prada and Channel, he could tell that they were high maintenance and way out of his league. He was going to have to play it cool if he wanted to hook up with one of them -- and he definitely wanted to.

"Hey ladies, y'all smoke?" he said as he fired up a blunt, leaning back and trying to look cool as possible.

"Me and Star do," the light-skinned girl with the hazel eyes replied.

"But Cahmel and Cahmely don't." She pointed, referring to the twins.

"But we do drink," the twins said at the same time.

"Don't trip on that, ladies. I got something new for y'all," Solo said as he got six glasses from behind the bar and lined them up in a row.

He poured Patron and Nuvo in each glass.

"They call this the Jimmy Neutron and it will definitely take you to outer space, first class," he said with a big smile.

He gave each of the girls a glass, and then he sat on the corner of the pool table.

"What's up with some music?" Star said as she hit the blunt and took a sip of her drink.

"They ain't got nothing for you to salsa to, girl," Hazel said, joking with Star about her Hispanic heritage.

"Girl, fuck you. You just mad cause you can't move like me, bitch."

Star got up and bounced her ass and they both began to laugh and high five each other. Blazz almost spilled his drink when he saw Star shake her ass. His mind was made up. He had to have her.

"I don't know how to work this shit," Blazz said, referring to the high tech surround sound system. "Where Mack ass at? The nigga taking a shit or something?" Solo asked Blazz as he poured himself another drink at the bar.

"I don't know what the fuck he doing. He in the room."

Solo walked across the living room and knocked on the door, then walked in. Mack was lying on the bed, talking on the phone with Kat. He acknowledged Solo with a head nod.

"Babe, my cousin here. Let me holla at him, then I'm call you back, ok? Alright, bye,"

"What up, blood? Where the fuck you been, nigga? You act like you can't answer your phone and shit." Solo closed the door and sat down in a chair by the glass wall.

He looked down at the traffic going by and sipped his drink.

"Nigga, I been laying low. Shit was getting crazy. I had to get away and clear my head so I could plan my next move." Mack looked at his phone as he got a text.

"Man, guess who turned up dead while yo ass was on vacation, blood?"

T-Mack didn't answer. He just stared at Solo with a look that said 'spit it out'.

"My niggas Lil Man and Booboo." Solo paused and looked at T-Mack to find out how he took the news.

There was no change in Mack's expression, so Solo continued on.

"Lil Man's sister called me crying, asking all types of questions. When the last time I seen him and shit like that. The bitch been calling me all day. I don't even answer her calls anymore."

"Yeah, that's crazy," Mack said as he got of the bed and walked to the window.

He looked out at the world, lost in deep thought. Solo could tell by T-Mack's behavior that he knew way more about Lil Man and Booboo than he was leading on. He was hiding something. Solo wanted to pry, but knew it was best to just let it go. Whatever it was he knew Mack wasn't about to tell him, so he changed the subject.

"Nigga, did you see the bitches I brought with me? I told you they was fly. The twins that's all me, baby. I'm trying to fuck both of them at the same time. That ah be some shit to write home about, blood," Solo said as he stood up and smacked T-Mack playfully on the back.

"Where you find them at, nigga? They don't look like they from around here," Mack replied as he checked them out through the cameras.

He walked to the flat screen and looked closer at the screen they were on. Then he touched it with his finger and now there was just one picture covering the whole fifty-two inch TV. He could really see the girls now and they were beautiful.

"I was at this video shoot for Young Money when the light-skinned one, Hazel, asked if I knew where to get some smoke. I said, 'Is giraffe pussy out of reach?' The bitch started laughing and the next thing you know I got four bitches in my ride and ain't none of them from LA!"

Mack was impressed. Solo was a true ladies' man. The nigga weighed at least 300 pounds with dark skin and tattoos everywhere. He was the only nigga from the hood that had more tattoos then T-Mack. He looked like a real killa to say the least, but women still gravitated to him like he was a teddy bear.

"Let me back out there before Blazz try to move in on my two. Come on, nigga," Solo was saying as he opened the door and walked out.

Mack came out behind him. He had on a white tank top, blue jeans, white Nikes, a Gucci belt, two big diamond earrings and a diamond chain that went past the bottom of his chest. All four women stopped what they were doing and checked him out.

"Ladies."

He walked to the stereo, went through a playlist and selected a song by Rihanna. The Jamaican dancehall beat shook the apartment as Rihanna sang *Man down...Man down...*

All four girls began to move in their seats, then Star got up and began doing a Jamaican dance called the Slow Wind. She waved one hand high in the air while she turned her body in a circle, moving her hips from side to side. She noticed the way Blazz was watching her. They locked eyes and she danced over to where he was standing and began dancing with her butt up against him. He downed the last of his drink, sat the empty glass down and put one hand on each side of her hips. They began to move seductively. Across the room, everyone was enjoying the show they were putting on -- everyone, that is, except Hazel and T-Mack. Hazel had caught his eye. She stood out from the rest. There was something about her. It had to be those sexy eyes, Mack thought, as he walked across the room and sat on the couch next to her, firing up a fresh blunt.

"What up, ma? I hope you and your friends are having a good time," he said as he passed her the blunt.

"Yeah, we good. This is a nice place. Is it yours?" she said, coughing from the potent weed smoke.

"Yeah this me. You ok, though?"

Hazel was still coughing. She held up one hand for him. He patted her on the back to try and help. She finally stopped coughing and caught her breath.

"Damn! This shit is good!" she said with tears in her eyes. "Where you get this shit from?"

She passed him back the blunt and took a sip of her drink.

"I got a plug," was the only information he was about to give her. "So where y'all from?"

"We all from San Diego. We came down last night. We had to do a video shoot today."

"So you dancers? Models or strippers?"

He tried to pass her back the blunt. She shook her head no. She was high. If she hit the blunt again, she might pass out.

"I'm good. The twins Cahmel and Cahmely are models and they bring me and Star with them to shoots sometimes so we can make some extra money. But I'm in school for fashion design. That's where I met them. Star is my cousin."

"Yo cousin. So y'all like Puerto Rican or something? This yo real hair?" he said as he playfully pulled on her hair.

"Yeah, papee, it is."

She was smiling at him. Her eyes were so low, you could barely see her pupils.

"But we Dominican, not Puerto Rican. And what's your name, anyway?"

"T-Mack. And yours?"

Hazel was fine to say the least, and any nigga in Los Angeles would have been proud to have her on his arm. Mack could tell by the way she looked at him with those hazel eyes that he could have her, and that was definitely a boost for his already big ego. But he couldn't get Kat out of his mind. They had spent every day together for the last two weeks while he was laying low. She had his mind gone. Whenever they were apart, he missed her and couldn't wait to get back to her. And they had not even had sex yet.

In a way, he was scared to take the relationship to the next level. He already cared about her more than he had ever cared about any women except his mother and was afraid of what he really didn't know. Even now, as he sat next to Hazel, he couldn't get Kat off his mind.

Then his phone vibrated, which meant he had a text. He took it out the pouch and checked it, and it was Kat.

"Hey babe, I'm outside."

"Outside where? The shop?" Mack got up. "Excuse me, Hazel."

He walked to the bedroom and checked the cameras, and there it was parked on Crenshaw -- an all-white 650 convertible BMW. Kat was already out the car and at the front door. If she were any other female, she would have gotten cursed out for popping up unannounced and she would have never made it past the front door. But she wasn't any other female. She was Kathrin, the only female he ever cared about. So he reached up reluctantly and buzzed her in.

Kat walked through the front door of the shop. She really didn't know what she was doing there. She knew better then to pop up on a man without calling first, but when her and Mack were on the phone earlier and his cousin Solo walked in, she swore she heard female voices in the background. Before they hung up she had told Mack to call her right back, and that was forty-five minutes ago. Any other time Mack would have called or texted her. Something deep down inside her told her to go see what he was up to. She hoped it was nothing and she felt kind of silly acting so jealous. On the way over there she contemplated turning around several times but couldn't bring herself to do so. The last two weeks she had spent every day with him. She was hardly ever at home and she had lost her job at the club because she never showed up any more. Her and Sunshine rarely spoke. All her time was either spent with T-Mack or spent thinking about him.

As she walked up the steps, she could hear music and laughter coming from the other side of the door. She stood there waiting to be buzzed in. T-Mack opened the door and let Kat in. He gave her a hug and kissed her on the mouth.

The room was quiet now except for the music playing. For a moment everyone stopped what they were doing and stared at Kat, especially Hazel. Kat returned their glares with a look that said, "I know one of you ho's thought you came up, but this nigga belongs to me." Mack could feel the room heating up, so he took Kat's hand and led her to the room. Hazel watched the couple as they disappeared through the doors, wishing it were her on the other side of the wall.

"So that's why you didn't call me back," Kat said as she turned around and looked T-Mack dead in the eyes.

He closed the door and reached out to her, but she stepped back and crossed her arms over her chest.

"Answer me, Travon. Is that why you didn't call back?"

He could tell Kat was really upset. He had not expected her to act this way. He really didn't see what the problem was. He was not doing anything and he was not planning to, but Kat obviously thought different.

"I saw the way that light-skinned bitch was looking at me. I should go fuck that ho up. How the fuck you gone try to play me like this, T?"

She couldn't believe she let herself be fooled by him. She thought he cared. She just knew he was different. She grabbed her purse off the bed and tried to pass by Mack so she could leave. He grabbed her by the arm.

"Let me go, T. I'm leaving." She struggled to get free, but then he wrapped his arms around her and held her tight.

"Listen ma. Wait one second and just listen, goddamn it."

"No, I don't want to hear it," she said as she struggled to get free from his powerful arms.

"Babe."

"Don't babe me, nigga."

"Babe. Look. I wasn't doing shit. Solo brought them over here to smoke, that's it. I swear to god, ma." He was still holding her tight, afraid to let her go.

"You must think I'm a fool." She was crying now, tears running down her face and soaking his shirt.

He felt his heart ache. "Look ma, I don't want none of those bitches, babe. They ain't got nothing on you. I love you, babe."

He couldn't believe his ears and neither could Kat, but he meant every word he said. He was in love with her and there was no turning back. She stopped resisting his hold and looked up at him with tears in her eyes.

"I love you too, babe," she said.

He leaned his head down and kissed her. She parted her lips and let his tongue slide in. They began to kiss each other passionately. She pulled him backwards until they hit the bed and fell back. He began kissing and sucking on her neck.

She let out a sound of pleasure. "Oh, babe."

As he went lower and lower, she put her hands on top of his head and pushed his face into her cleavage. He pulled her shirt down with one hand and unfastened her bra with the other. Her breasts burst out. He gently took one in his hand and brought it up to his mouth and began to lick and suck on the nipple.

"Mmmmmm, babe." She moaned and began to grind against him. Her skirt started riding up her thighs till it was around her waist. As he licked and sucked from breast to breast and nipple to nipple, he reached down and pulled her panties off, then slid one finger in her wetness. All at once, juices began to run down his hand and her thighs.

"Yes, daddy. Ooh yes," she moaned in a low sexy voice.

She reached for his belt and fumbled with it until it finally came off. She reached down and grabbed his manhood. It swelled in her hand until it was rock hard and throbbing.

She licked her lips and whispered in his ear. "I want you now, daddy."

He kicked his pants and boxers off and climbed up between her legs. He looked her in the eyes as he slowly went in deep, filling her wet, silky, hot love spot to capacity.

"Ohhhhh, yes. Oh my god," she yelled out in pleasure.

He wrapped his arm around her as he pounded in and out, back and forth, side to side. She felt so good to him. He could barely control himself.

"You like that?"

"Oh yes, daddy. Don't stop!"

He began pumping harder and faster.

"Oh shit, daddy. Oh shit, I'm about to cum. Oh my god!"

They both let go and exploded like a nuclear bomb, juices everywhere, all over the bed. They both lay there trying to catch their breaths. She crawled on top of him and laid her head on his chest. She began to make small circles with her tongue on his skin and he felt himself begin to rise again.

Blazz kept staring at his brother as they drove through traffic. Mack had hardly said a word to him. His mind seemed preoccupied. He did not even complain when Blazz had asked him to drop Star off at her room. He didn't even ask Blazz how far he got with her. Something wasn't right with the nigga today, Blazz thought.

"What the fuck is wrong with you, nigga? You acting all weird and shit."

"I'm good bro," Mack said as they pulled in the parking lot of the Mercedes Benz dealership in downtown LA.

He parked the truck and got out. "I'll be right back."

Ten minutes later he came back to the truck. "Look, nigga. I want you to follow me to the condo. They finally got my car ready. They should be bringing it out right now."

"You about to let me drive the Escalade? Yo nigga, I know you tripping right now."

Blazz climbed across the center to the driver's seat. He couldn't believe T-Mack was about to let him drive his brand new truck, especially after he had already crashed more than a few cars that his brother bought for him. This was his chance to show Mack that he knew how to drive better now and he was hoping that if he did good, maybe Mack would let him borrow one of his cars sometime.

The repairman brought the Benz around. T-Mack got in and drove off with Blazz following behind him, driving as carefully as possible. Twenty minutes later they pulled through the gates at T-Mack's condo.

CHAPTER 11

Mack parked the Benz and got out. He walked to the window of the truck. "Park it over there, bro," Mack said, pointing to an empty parking stall three cars down.

Blazz slowly pulled into the space that was a little small for the truck, but he made it in with no problem. He was relieved that he had not messed up anything. Then, just as he was about to apply the brake, the truck abruptly came to a stop on its own with a loud cracking sound.

CRACK...

"Damn, this nigga's going kill me," he said to himself out loud.

He slowly got out of the truck and went to the front to look at the damage. He ran into a pole and put a crack in the middle of the bumper. It was not bad, but his brother was never going to let him drive again. At the thought of that, he looked around to see why T-Mack was not cursing his ass out. He was nowhere in sight. He had gone into the house before Blazz hit the pole. Blazz knew he had to do something before Mack found out. He pulled out his cell phone and dialed his homeboy Lee Lee. The phone rang three times, then someone answered.

"Hello?"

It was a girl's voice. She sounded irritated and you could hear a baby crying in the background.

"Yeah, is Leelee there?"

"Who is this?" she yelled into the phone.

Blazz wanted to check the girl, but out of respect to his homie he held his tongue.

"This Blazz."

"Hold on." She slammed the phone down and called out for Leelee.

"Leelee! This nigga Blazz on the phone, babe!"

"Ok, I got it in here," he yelled back, picking up the phone in the bedroom and putting Grand Theft on pause.

"What up, Blazz. What's good with you, blood?"

"Shit, my nigga. Man, I need yo help, dawg. I…"

"Hold on, blood… Bitch, hang up the phone! I can hear your noisy ass," Leelee yelled to his girl.

"I was about to, nigga! Ain't nobody trying to listen to y'all," she yelled as she hung up.

"A nigga can't get no privacy around this bitch…Now what was you saying, blood?" Leelee said as he unpaused the game and began to play.

"I need a front bumper cover off a black Escalade. A new one."

"I can do that, dawg. Shit, give me like two days and I'll have that shit in my garage."

Blazz could not wait two days. By then Mack would have noticed the crack in his bumper and flipped out on him. His chances of using the truck again would be out the window.

"Naw, nigga I need that shit tonight, dawg. I fucked Mack's truck up and I got to get that shit fixed before he find out." Blazz was pacing back and forth in the parking lot.

"Damn nigga. Mack crazy ass gone fuck you up, blood," Leelee said as he started to laugh.

Blazz didn't find anything funny.

"Look dawg, can you help me or not? Cause if not, I'm call someone else."

"Calm down, blood. I got you, but you gone have to help me. So slide by my pad at midnight and we will go get that and put it on before the sun come up."

"Ok, I'll be there. Good looking, dawg."

"No problem. Just have my paper. Five hundred cash, no credit," he joked as he hung up the phone.

Blazz put his phone away and headed upstairs to get ready for to-night, praying that his brother would not discover the damage to his truck.

Later on that night, a blue Lexus pulled up to a one-story house on 57th Street. There were three young men hanging out in the yard. They all paused and looked at the car suspiciously as it came to a stop in front of the house. One of the guys, a medium built guy with long hair that went down his back, pulled out a colt 45 and held it to his side ready to open fire.

"Who the fuck is that, blood?" he said to the others.

Before they could respond, Leelee came out the back dressed in all black with three screwdrivers and a pair of gloves hanging out his back pocket, talking on his cell phone.

"Here I come. That's you in the Lexus?"

Blazz sat behind the wheel of a GS 400. He had stolen it from the neighborhood that surrounded his brother's condo so he could get to Cheek's house.

"Yeah, nigga, but this shit stolen so we got to take yo car."

"Man, fuck that shit. We gonna ride in this shit," he said as he slipped his gloves on.

He opened the passenger door, got in and checked out the car.

"Damn, this shit is tight, dawg. If you can steal this shit, what you need me for?"

"Man, you know I only know how to knock Jap shit, nigga. That American shit is way too hard."

As they pulled off, Leelee yelled out the window to his homies.

"Blood, I'll see y'all later and leave the burner with my baby mama if you leave."

They turned the corner onto Central headed for Slauson Blvd.

"Where you think we should go, dawg?" Blazz said as he turned the corner headed west.

Leelee thought for a moment before he answered.

"Let's go to Hollywood. Yeah, niggas be parking all on the streets, while they ass in the club getting fucked up. We gonna be outside taking they shit," he said with a smile.

Blazz liked the idea. They could easily find a new Escalade in Hollywood. There were a lot of cops, but Leelee was good. He was really good. He could steal a car with lightning speed. He once stole a car in front of a furniture store after following the owner there. He had the car started up before the owner even walked through the front door of the store.

Blazz met Leelee through his brother T-Mack. Leelee and Mack were from the same hood, Blood Stone Villains. Leelee was from 56 Street and Mack was from 52 Street. Leelee was the same age as Mack. He was medium built, about 5'8". He weighed 160 pounds with light brown skin and long hair. He loved to smoke weed and steal cars. Blazz had smoked his first blunt with him in Lee Lee's garage. Then they had gone out and Leelee showed him how to steal his first car.

They had been driving around Hollywood for thirty minutes looking up and down streets and in parking lots. They had seen every kind of car from Bugs to Bentleys, but no Escalades. Both men were getting restless, but they both knew it was just a matter of time.

"Hold up, blood. Turn around. I think I saw one right down that street."

Leelee quickly turned around and headed towards the other street, then turned up the block. Leelee was directing him as they turned the corner. They both spotted the truck.

"Bingo!" both said at the same time.

They were excited and ready to get the truck and get out of there.

"Pull right up on the side of it and I'm hop out and do my thang. You just watch out, blood."

Blazz pulled the Lexus up to the truck and as Leelee was about to get out, he noticed there was a man sitting in the driver's seat leaning back, talking on a cell phone.

"Pull off, dawg. It's a white boy in the truck."

"Damn, dawg. What the fuck you want to do? Let's go park down the street and wait for him to get out."

Blazz was anxious. He wanted to get the whole thing over with. As he was about to turn around, he noticed a light blinking, indicating the fuel was low.

"Fuck dawg. We got to find a gas station."

Leelee looked over at the gauge, then back at the truck.

"Fuck that shit, blood. Go around the corner and pull behind him. We gonna get this bitch ass nigga first."

Blazz drove around the corner and pulled right behind the Escalade.

"We gone sit right here until this nigga get the fuck out and walk off. I ain't trying to be looking for trucks all night."

It was getting late and people were starting to slowly come out of the clubs most of them would be closing in thirty minutes. They were running out of time.

"This nigga need to hurry the fuck up. What the fuck is he waiting on?" Blazz complained.

He was running out of patience. Just as he was about to suggest they look somewhere else, the Escalade started up and the man was about to pull off.

"The nigga 'bout to leave, blood. If you want that shit, you better run into the back of it," Leelee said, laughing.

Blazz did not see what was funny, but he was used to Leelee bizarre sense of humor.

"What's running into the back of the truck going to do, dawg?" Blazz asked annoyed.

"Nigga, just do it, blood."

Blazz didn't know what Leelee had planned, but the truck was about to leave, so he was running out of time. He had to make a choice. He quickly started up the Lexus and ran it into the back of the truck. The white guy turned the truck off and got out yelling.

Blazz didn't know what the plan was, so he said, "Now what?" as he looked over at the empty passenger seat.

The passenger door was open, but Leelee was nowhere in sight. Blazz was hot. He could not believe Leelee's ass ran out on him. The white man was banging on the window, demanding an explanation. Just as Blazz was about to get out the car and check the man, the Escalade started up with a low rumble and Leelee stuck his head out the window.

"Come on, blood…..ha ha!" He pulled off laughing.

Blazz just shook his head. He should have known better than to think his boy would leave him behind. He looked at the man standing at the door holding his keys up with a look of bewilderment on his face. He was still trying to figure out how his truck had been stolen in less than sixty seconds when Blazz took off so fast in pursuit of Leelee that he almost ran the man's foot over.

Both vehicles made it to the freeway and headed for T-Mack's house.

⋏

Mack woke up with the smell of breakfast cooking in the air. Kat was not lying when she told him she knew how to cook. She was a great cook and had proven it to him several times in the last few weeks. They were spending all their free time together. Mack would only leave her if he had to take care of some business with Solo. He would be gone for a couple of hours, then he would rush back home to her as soon as he was done. They were in love. He had never felt this way about anyone. The closer they grew together, the further Kat and Sunshine grew apart. Mack never liked Sunshine. He knew what type of girl she was and he knew she was not to be trusted, so he never let Kat bring her to the house. Plus he and Kat were always out eating at restaurants or at the movies. They even took a day trip to Disneyland. Things were going great.

The phone rang, snapping him out of his thoughts.

"Hello?" he said as he put the phone to his ear.

"What up, bro?" It was Blazz calling from an 818 number Mack did not recognize.

"What the fuck you doing in the Valley, blood? I thought you was on the Eastside, bro?"

"Um yeah. Well I was, but I got caught up in some bullshit. Umm… I'm in jail."

"Nigga, you ain't in jail, cause you would have been calling collect, stupid mutha fucka," Mack said as he got out of bed and headed for the kitchen.

Kat was standing at the stove with her hair clipped up in a bun and she was wearing one of Mack's white T-shirts that fit her like a dress coming down to her knees. He kissed her on the forehead and slapped her on the ass.

"Nigga, you still there?" Blazz yelled through the phone.

Mack was temporarily distracted by the sight of Kat.

"Yeah, blood, but I don't got time for your games, nigga…" Blazz cut him off before he could finish.

"Nigga, I'm not playing. I'm in Juvenile Hall, man. For a GTA. I got caught in a stolen Lexus at like four-thirty this morning. I need a lawyer, bro. I been calling my mom's, but she not answering her phone."

Blazz was scared. He had never been locked up before and did not know what to expect. After he and Leelee stole the struck, they went to Mack's house and switched the bumpers. It took about an hour after that they got rid of the stolen Escalade and Blazz dropped Cheeks back off at his house. Then he was planning on going to Mack's shop to spend the night, but instead he got in a high-speed chase with LAPD, crashed the Lexus and ended up in Juvenile Hall.

Chapter 12

Mack couldn't believe Blazz was still running the streets and breaking the law after everything he had been doing for him. Mack had been trying his hardest to keep Blazz out of trouble and keep him in school and on the football team where Blazz excelled. He was the starting wide receiver and the top ten colleges were already aggressively trying to recruit him, but Blazz was constantly getting into trouble at school and with the law. He was already on probation and this might be the last straw. Mack didn't know if he could save him.

"Man, bro, don't worry. I'm call my lawyer and find out where your mom's at so we can get you out of there, little nigga." Mack hung up the phone and by the look on his face, Kat could tell something was wrong.

"Is everything ok, babe?" she said as she began fixing him a plate.

Mack sat down at the table and tried to clear his head so he could plan his next move.

"Blazz is in Juvenile Hall. He got caught in a stolen car."

Kat stopped what she was doing and went and sat on Mack's lap. She put her arms around his neck and looked him in his eyes. She knew how much he loved his little brother and she knew he felt responsible for him so he had to be taking this hard.

"He's going to be ok. Blazz is tough. Don't blame yourself. You did everything you could to try and keep him out of trouble."

"I know, babe, but I just wish he would have listened to me instead of trying to be like me. I can't help but feel that this shit is my fault."

"You did the best you could."

Mack was happy Kat was there to help him through this. He knew his brother was locked up, but he would do whatever it took to get him out. He tried calling his lawyer twice and got no answer, so he left a message letting him know it was urgent. He reached Blazz's mother and let her know what had happened.

"Travon, I don't know what I'm going to do with that boy. He just don't listen to me. He's so damn hardheaded. The judge told him the next time he saw him in his courtroom, he was going to throw the book at him."

"Yeah, I know, Miss Jackson. That's why I'm going to give my lawyer your number. He's really good and I think he can help. He should be calling you sometime today, ok? His name is Robert Swagner."

"Boy, I can't afford no lawyer. I can barely get by as it is."

"Oh no, I got it. You don't have to pay anything."

"Thank you, Travon, but you don't have to do that. You're not the boy's father."

"I know, but I want to help and I wouldn't feel right if they gave him a long time knowing that I could have done something about it. Plus he's my little brother. He's my responsibility too."

Miss Jackson knew T-Mack loved his brother. That's why he was always trying to step up and be the father her son never really had. She really did not want T-Mack to spend his money on a lawyer, but she did want her son home and this might be the only chance he had. She reluctantly agreed.

"Ok, Travon. I really appreciate everything you have done for that boy. Thank you."

"Calling case number 4256 on the court docket. The people of the State of California verses Brian Mack. Will the defendant please rise."

Blazz stood up. He had been locked up for a month already and he was happy to see everyone had come to his court date. His mother, T-Mack and even Kat had all showed up to show their support. The lawyer Mack had gotten him was really good. The judge wanted to send Blazz to CYA, a prison for adolescents, for 3 years, but Mack's lawyer Mr. Swagner postponed the case and went to work on getting his sentence lowered.

Robert Swagner was a tall, slim, forty-year-old, half-Italian, half-German, white man. He wore tailor-made suits, designer shoes and was a fast talker. He was born and raised in Philadelphia, but had been living in Los Angeles for the last ten years. He was connected to everyone -- judges, police chiefs and the DA on one side, and drug dealers, hit men, cartels and gang members on the other side. If anyone could get Blazz out of the situation, it would be him.

He stood up with a look on his face that said he would rather be somewhere else. He knew what the DA was going to do. The case was no big deal to him. He usually did not even take juvenile cases, but his relationship with Mack went beyond client and attorney, so he had agreed to take the case.

"Robert Swagner on behalf of Brian Mack." He sat back down and the DA stood up.

"Jim Mathews on behalf of the State."

The DA was a young white man. He had been working the courts for just a few years, but had already put away his fair share of young minorities. The judge was a fifty-something-year-old Korean man who loved his job. He felt while working the juvenile courts he could serve the community better by catching the problem early before it got out of hand. He was filling in for Judge Snider, the judge who had promised to send Blazz away the next time he stepped foot in his court.

"Are both parties ready to proceed?" the judge said.

He looked over the top of his reading glasses at both men. They both answered yes.

"Ok then. Well, I have here in front of me Mr. Mack's case file. It seems he's been in this courtroom a few times for some minor infractions and is certainly on formal probation for narcotics possession. I also have his probation officer's report." The judge stopped talking and searched for the report.

"Yes, here it is. His probation officer indicated that he has been reporting every month, paying his fines on time and has not had a dirty test in over a year. But the case you are here for today is serious, to say the least."

The judge was about to start going over the case, but before he could begin, Mr. Swagner stood up and asked to approach the bench. The judge did not like being cut off, but allowed both lawyers to approach.

"Your honor, Mr. Mathews and I have come to an agreement which will allow Mr. Mack to stay in custody until completion of his high school diploma. After completion, he will be released to the custody of his mother who is present in court today. My client realizes what he did was wrong. He has several colleges that are offering him full scholarships. Both the DA and myself agree that sending him to CYA will do more harm than good. It will not only ruin his chances of going to college, but could turn him into a harder criminal."

The judge looked at Blazz, then at the DA.

"Is this the agreement you made with Mr. Swagner? And have you talked it over with the defendant?"

"Yes, your honor. In light of his scholarships and his clean probation report, I do believe he deserves one more chance. I already let him know this is it. He will be eighteen in seven months, so he knows there are no more chances after this one, sir."

Mack sat in the back of the courtroom with Miss Jackson and Kat. He knew what they were up there discussing. Everything had been worked out the day before over lunch with the DA. Mack paid the bill -- thirty thousand dollars cash. Like his mom always said when she was alive, it's not what you know, it's who you know. And his lawyer knew everyone.

"Well, I see no reason to go against the deal. Okay, everyone get back to their seats so we can get this on record."

And just like that, Blazz was off the hook. All he had to do was get his high school diploma, for which he already had most of his credits, and he would be back home.

Mack drove down the street with Kat in silence thinking about what he was going to do with his brother once he came home. The truth was there were no scholarships waiting on him. Once the schools found out about his arrest, they lost all interest in Blazz. Between his poor work effort and this new criminal case, he was just too much of a risk. No school wanted to have anything to do with him when there were plenty of other young talented athletes with no criminal records to choose from. Mack had a hard decision to make. He knew what he had to do. When Blazz came home he was going to have to take him under his wing and teach him everything he knew about the game. He did not want to bring his little brother into a life of crime, but he felt he was headed that way anyway, so he might as well learn from the best.

"It's ok, babe. He will be home soon and you got me to keep you busy until then." Kat was trying to cheer him up.

She could see her man was bothered by this whole ordeal. She had never seen him like this. She wished there was something she could do to make that smile appear on his face that she had come to love.

"I'm good, babe. I'm just thinking, that's all."

"About what?"

"Everything... Like what I'm going do with my bad ass little bro. I think it's time I slow down a little. I know you done figured out that I'm not no boxer."

He glanced at her as he turned into the alley behind his shop. While they waited for the gate to open, she turned in her seat to face him.

"Yeah, I realized that a long time ago, but I figured you would tell me when you were ready."

That was one of the things he loved about Kat. She was different than most females. She wasn't nosy. She respected his privacy and did not ask a lot of questions. She just sat back and observed like a student, watching and learning from a teacher.

As they walked into the upstairs apartment over the shop, Mack headed straight for the bar and grabbed a bottle of Moscato, then put it back and grabbed the Belvedere, deciding he was going to need something a little stronger. He took two glasses off the shelf and filled them halfway. He grabbed some cranberry juice and headed for the couch. As he sat down by Kat, she took the juice from his hand and began to pour it from one glass into the other. Mack watched the two liquids mix together lost in thought, then he raised the glass to his lips and took a big drink, nearly empting the whole thing.

"Well, it's really not that complicated, but it is something that needs to stay between us."

He paused for a second and looked her in the eyes to make sure she understood that what he was about to reveal to her was serious. She could tell by the look on his face that it was so. She just shook her head yes and took the first sip of her drink. The alcohol burned her throat and chest as it went down, so she added a little more juice to it.

"Well, when I was younger, I got busted for a robbery and got sent to CYA. After I had been there for a year, I met this little Italian boy. At first I really did not like the guy. He was always running off at the mouth like he was John Gotti or somebody ……" Mack was smiling as he recalled the first time he met Geno.

"Anyways, there were a few skinheads on our cell block that couldn't stand Geno due to the fact that he was always hanging out with blacks. So one day at shower time, they tried to make a move on him. There were six blacks in the shower, babe. Tiny Bone from 20's, Zig-Zag from Swan's, Big Jack from my hood, Red Flag from Families, one nigga from Oakland and myself. All of us were bloods, except the nigga from Oakland, but he ran with us. There were three skinheads in the shower and I could tell something was up, because usually they would be talking and joking with each other but not this day. They were all quiet and one looked really nervous. At first I thought they were going to maybe make a move on us or something. Then Geno came in the shower and I could tell he was the target. There was only one shower open and it was between me and one of the white boys. His name was Sledgehammer. He stood about 6'8" and weighed about 250 pounds. The boy was bench-pressing 450 and he was seventeen years old. He was also the shot caller for every skinhead on the yard.

"Geno came and put his clean clothes down on the bench. He grabbed his wash towel and soap and got in between us. Now even though Geno had a big mouth, he was far from a big dude. He was about 5'7" and skinny as hell.

He couldn't weigh more than 140 pounds soaking wet. So he starts soaping up and running off at the mouth, talking about why was it so fucking quiet in here and did somebody die. Then before we knew it, Sledgehammer turns and grabs Geno from the back and puts him in a chokehold. Then the other two white boys grab his legs off the ground. So now Geno's whole body is up in the air. He was trying to yell, but Sledgehammer was choking the shit out of him. Me and the homies started to dry off so we could get out of the way. The shit really had nothing to do with us. Even though Geno fucked with us, he was still white, so it really was none of our business. Whites ran with whites and blacks ran with blacks and Mexicans ran with Mexicans. That's just the way it is in prison. Even in CYA.

"So Geno keeps reaching for his wash towel and finally he gets a hold of it. And boom, out of the towel he pulls out this box cutter and slashes one of the white boys holding his legs across the face. Blood starts running down his face and he starts screaming. The other fool holding his legs drops him and tries to step back, but before he could move, Geno slashes him twice. Once to the face and once to the chest. Now blood is everywhere. It starts to look like a scene from a horror movie. By now, me and my niggas is dressed and about to go back to our cells, when I see Geno's arm go limp and drop the box cutter. Then Sledgehammer lets him go and Geno's body drops to the shower floor. Sledgehammer had choked him until he passed out.

"Now this gay ass nigga started pulling on his dick, getting it all hard and shit. Then he started to roll Geno over on to his stomach so his ass would be exposed. And that's when I had enough and said fuck it. So I turned and I tell Sledgehammer that Geno with us and that I couldn't let him do whatever the fuck he thought he was about to do. So he steps up to me and starts laughing and tells me if I don't get the fuck out of his face I would be next. Now mind you, my boys were halfway down the hall by now and his boys were fuckin' bleeding to death and Geno was still out cold. So it was basically just me and him and this fool was 50 pounds heavier and three inches taller than me. So I guess he thought he could take me. As I turn like if I was about to leave, then he drops his guard, so I spent back around and hit him with a fast right and then a left hook to his jaw. Man, I hit him so hard you could hear his jaw break. He hit the ground hard. He was out cold.

"Geno started to wake up, so I helped him off the floor. Then five guards came busting in. Man, they mace the shit out of us. They rushed the three white boys to the informatory and left me and Geno handcuffed to the bench in the showers. Geno's ass was still naked. We was both covered in blood, eyes burning, skin on fire. They left us like that for three hours. I'll never forget that shit. They threw us in the hole for six months for that shit. We were cellmates the whole time so we became good friends. Geno told me how his family was rich and that his uncle and dad were from the mob. Now, I didn't believe none of this shit, but it was boring as fuck in the hole, so I just listened to the bullshit to keep me entertained.

"So Geno goes home first. I give him my number and the address to my grandma's house and we make plans to fuck with each other when I get out. So after being locked up for four years, I finally get released. One day I'm sitting on the porch with my little bro and this white 600 Benz pulls up to my house. Geno hops out the driver's seat dressed like a used cars salesman, hair all slicked back, talking 'bout 'What's up, bro?'

"At first I didn't even recognize him. It had been a few years since I saw him and he had grown up. Once I knew who it was, I ran down and gave the fool a hug. We relived old times and then he tells me that he's working for his family, making all kinds of money. Now if he had not pulled up in a brand new 600 Benz, I probably would have thought he was full of shit, but the proof was in the pudding and that ride was worth a whole lot of pudding. So he tells me that he told his uncle all about me and how I saved his ass literally and that he wants to meet me and thank me personally. And if everything goes well, he would give me a job working for the family. So I'm like fuck it, 'Where he at?' And he was like, 'In the back seat of the car.' So we both walk up to the car and Geno opens the back door and motions for me to get in. I climb in and sit down. The guy looks me up and down and says, 'You're the guy that saved lil Geno's ass, huh?' I shake my head yes. Then he asked me if I like money. I say, 'Hell yeah, I like money.' So he's like, 'Look kid. I like you and I like what you did for my nephew. So here's what I'm going to do for you.

I'm going to give you a job.' I say, 'Doing what?' He looks at me and smiles and says, 'Whatever the fuck I want you to do. You got a problem with that?' I told him, as long as I'm getting paid, hell naw.

"So the next night Geno calls me and tells me to be ready in twenty minutes. He's coming to pick me up. Twenty minutes later he pulls up to my house in a white Chevy van. He honks the horn and I come outside. I walk to the van and get in. I smell gas, so I'm like, 'What's up, blood? What we got to do? I'm broke as fuck and I need some money.' He's like, 'Man, you don't never got to worry about money again. After you do this one thing, you're in.'

"So we drive to Santa Monica and go to this classic car dealership and we get out at the gate and pull the van in. We grab some gas containers out the back and start pouring gas on all the cars and then on the building. Then we drove back out the gate. Geno gave me a lighter. I flicked it until a flame came on and I locked it in place so it would not turn off. Then I threw it at one of the gas-covered cars and the shit caught fire fast. The next thing you know, the whole place was up in flames.

"We drive off and Geno pulls back up to my house. He tells me he will call me the next day. I'm like, 'Fuck that. When am I going to get paid?' He starts laughing and says, 'Man, I told you, you don't have to worry about money no more.' Then he drives off.

"Now I didn't hear from Geno for a whole week. I'm pissed off, telling my little bro what I'm going to do to him when I see him. Then Geno pulls up in a silver 745 BMW on 22" three-piece rims. I run up on him, ready to fuck his ass up, but before I could do anything, he throws me the keys and asks me how I like my new car. I'm like, 'Nigga, don't bullshit me.' He's like, 'I'm not bullshitting. Get in.' I get in and he opens up the glove compartment and hands me the pink slip to the car. The shit had my name on it. I didn't even have a license yet, but here I was the owner of an eight thousand dollar car. He hands me a cell phone and ten thousand dollars and tells me whenever he or his uncle calls, I needed to answer the phone and be ready for whatever. There was no turning back.

"And that's basically what I do. Whatever his uncle needs me to do. No questions asked. No matter what it is. Over the years, that's been a lot of things that I rather not and cannot discuss, but Geno was not lying when he said I never had to worry about money again. And, oh yeah. The man in the back seat of the car. His uncle…He's also my lawyer, Robert Swagner."

Kat did not know what to say. She had a thousand questions running through her mind.

"So, you're like in the mafia or something?"

Mack got up to fix himself another drink. He felt like getting really drunk. Something he rarely did, but tonight he wanted to cut loose.

"No, it's nothing like that. I don't think Rob is in the mafia. I think he just knows a lot of powerful people and they need things done and they come to him to handle it. I never meet anyone else but him and Geno, that's it."

"Do you trust him?"

Kat was a little scared by the whole mob thing. She had seen her fare share of gangster movies and they were always turning on each other. She didn't want anything to happen to Travon. He was becoming a big part of her life.

"Naw, babe I don't trust no one."

Kat climbed on his lap and pressed her lips against his neck.

"Not even me?" she said in a low, seductive voice.

He turned his head to face her so he could look her in the eye.

"Do you love me?" he asked her.

"Yes, babe. You know I do."

"Would you ever lie to me?"

"No babe, never."

Their eyes were locked and the apartment seemed to go perfectly silent. The Belvedere was taking full effect on both their minds.

"Would you ever keep secrets from me?"

The question made her break their stare. Her eyes fell to the floor and a single tear rolled down her left cheek.

"Everyone has a secret, babe, but I would never do anything to hurt you. Never."

She wanted to tell him she worked at a strip club and all the bad things she went through as a child, but she didn't know how. He had just shared something with her that could get him killed, so she felt she owed him something.

"Well, there is something I have been meaning to tell you."

She took a deep breath.

"Well, you know my girl Meka and me use to work at a club. I only did it for a month, babe and I never gave no lap dances or anything like that. I just didn't know how to tell you… I didn't want you to think I was a ho or a gold digger because it was not even like that."

Mack stared at her with a blank expression that she could not read. Then he pulled her close to him. He was happy that she had come clean. He knew Kat had not worked there long and had stopped once they stared dating. He just wanted to see how long she was going to keep it from him.

"You don't have to cry, babe. Everything's ok. I'm not tripping. You told me on your own and I believe you when you said you just waitressed, so relax, babe."

"So you not mad?"

Mack pressed his lips to hers. She parted her lips so she could receive his tongue and they began to kiss passionately. She put one leg on each side of them and they began to slowly grind against each other. Kat was on her second glass of vodka and Mack was on his fourth, so both their heads were spinning. They were both in another world. She began pulling his belt loose. Once it was out the way, she reached in his pants and grabbed his manhood. She felt it throbbing in her hand. Mack pulled one of her breasts free from her blouse and began to suck on her nipples while he reached under her skirt with his other hand. He began to rub on her pussy until he had her panties soaking wet.

Kat let out a low moan. "Mmmm…"

She raised up, pulled her panties to the side and began to rub the head of his dick across her wetness. She slowly lowered herself down on him. When she felt him enter her body, she let out another moan.

"Mmmmmm, babe."

Mack put both hands on her ass and began to thrust, going deep inside her, at the same time keeping with her riding rhythm. She could feel Mack deep inside her and she could feel herself start to shake and lose control. She wrapped her arms around his neck and held on tight while he hit her spot harder and harder over and over again until she couldn't take it any longer.

"Ooohhhh shit, daddy. I'm about to cum. Damn, babe."

Kat's insides exploded with pleasure. Then Mack turned her over and took her from the back. He held on to her waist with both hands while he slammed into her over and over. Kat could barely handle the sex he was giving her. She grabbed a pillow off the couch and bit down on it, letting out a muffled scream.

"Ohhhhh fuck!" Mack couldn't hold out any longer.

Kat's love spot felt so good. He began to pound away frantically. Then he let go and unloaded all he had stored inside him.

Now his whole body went limp as he collapsed on top of her. Their bodies were glistening with sweat and they were out of breath. Before you knew it, both of them were fast asleep.

CHAPTER 13

The next day across town, Solo was sitting in his Challenger warming it up in the driveway. He had his head down while he went through his iPod searching for something to listen to. Then he heard a car pull in behind him. He looked up in the rearview mirror to see who could be stopping by his house at eight in the morning without calling first. It was a white Ford Crown Vic with limo tint on all the windows. Seven antennas were on the truck and it had government plates. But even without the plates and antennas, he would have known by the tint alone that the vehicle belonged to the cops. He just didn't know which division, but he had a feeling that he would be finding out.

The driver and passenger doors opened up simultaneously and a male and female officer stepped out dressed in plain clothes. The female driver had on black slacks and a white blouse that was tucked in, revealing a gold badge on her belt. She had her long black hair pulled back in a ponytail. By the way she dressed and wore her hair, Solo could tell she was trying to downplay her looks, but there was no hiding the fact that she was beautiful.

They approached his car from both sides. The male officer tapped on the window using his badge. He was at least twenty years older than the female officer. Solo put him at around fifty. He was slightly overweight and going bald, but for some reason had decided to hang on to a few strands of blond hair on the side of his otherwise bald head. His clear blue eyes stared down. Solo had a feeling there was a lot going on behind those baby blues. He slowly reached for the button to roll the window down.

"Yes, can I help you?" He looked back and forth from the female officer to the male.

The man spoke first. "Well, I hope you can. Are you Michael Thomas?"

At first he thought about lying, but he figured if they knew where he lived, they probably also knew that he was in fact Michael Jamal Thomas.

"Yes, that's me. What can I do for you, officer?"

"Well, if you don't mind, can you please step out the car so we can ask you a few questions, sir?"

Solo thought about what he wanted to do for a moment. He knew he was way too big to run and his car was blocked in. Plus they knew who he was already. So he opened the passenger door and slowly got out.

Detective Mark Looner walked around and stood by his partner, Samantha. You could see the car raise up several inches when it no longer had to support Solo's six foot four, 300 pound, intimidating frame. It didn't help that he was covered in tattoos. Officer Looner instantly stepped back and rested his right hand on his gun. Solo took notice and smiled.

"Easy now cow boy," he said playfully.

But Looner didn't laugh or even smile. He just started talking.

"This is Detective Vicenta from LAPD Robbery and Homicide. I'm Detective Mark Looner from LA County Sheriff's Department."

He stopped and let that information sink in while he studied Solo's face for signs that he knew what they were there for.

It was Solo's turn to put his poker face on. He knew he could not give them any reason to dig into his business, so he tried to play it cool.

"What can I help you with? I don't know no one who got robbed or murdered recently."

Now Detective Samantha Vicenta spoke.

"Look, Michael. Do you mind if I call you Michael?"

She was turning on the charm, trying to break the tension so they could get as much information from him as possible.

"You can call me whatever you like, Detective. Just don't call me no suspect," Solo said, laughing while trying his hardest to seem relaxed.

"Call me Samantha. After all, we're here on a friendly visit. We just came to ask you a few questions."

"Ok, Samantha. What would you like to know?"

"Well, a few months ago in Hollywood, two people were killed. On that same night in Compton, two more people were murdered. One of them was Timothy White. Did you know Mr. White?"

"Who? Timothy White? Naw, I don't know nobody by that name."

"Well, maybe you knew him as Lil Man," Detective Looner said as he pulled a photo of Lil Man out and showed it to Solo.

"Oh yeah. I knew Lil Man. I don't know who killed him though."

"Well, his sister said he was supposed to meet up with you that night. Is that true?" Looner said as he pulled out another photo.

"This man was also with him and was murdered too. Do you know him, sir?"

Solo looked at the photo and handed it back.

"Yeah, that's Booboo. I knew him through Lil Man, and yeah, we was supposed to meet at the club. They wanted me to get them in because they didn't have no ID, that's all."

When Samantha heard him say 'club', she got a little excited.

"What club was this, Michael?"

"The club I was working at. Club Voodoo."

At the mention of the club's name, both detectives looked at each other. Detective Vicenta whipped out her notepad and began to scribble down a few words.

"So did they show up and did you get them in?"

"Yeah, they showed up early, around eight. I let them in through the back door and I saw them like maybe once or twice a little while after that, but that was it. There were like a few thousand people there. Voodoo is a big fucking club."

"So how long did you work there?"

Looner had a gut feeling that Solo knew more that he was letting on, but he knew they had nothing on him. He was going to have to do some more digging and maybe he would get lucky.

"Well, I really just worked there whenever they held special events that called for extra security."

"So you know that the owner and his girlfriend were also killed that night? They were the other two people we mentioned earlier. Did you know them, sir?"

"No, I never met them. Is that all? Cause I have somewhere I need to be."

Solo was getting tired of all the questions. He was getting a little nervous and just wanted to get away before he gave himself away.

"Well, here is my card. Please call if you hear anything, Michael."

"Yeah, I'll do that," Solo said as he took the card from Samantha's hand.

"We will be in touch," Looner said with the same blank look he had on his face when he first pulled up.

Solo watched as they drove off, then he pulled out his cell phone and called Mack. Mack's voicemail kept picking up, so he finally left a message.

"Nigga, call me ASAP. This some 911 shit, blood." He hung up.

He knew there was one more call he had to make.

CHAPTER 14

Mack woke up to the smell of bacon and eggs cooking in the kitchen. He had a terrible headache and his stomach was a little queasy.

"This is why I hate getting drunk. I feel like shit," he mumbled to himself as he rose up on the couch.

Kat, on the other hand, was feeling great. She hardly ever got hung over, but she knew her man did when he drank too much, so she had put on a pot of coffee earlier and began preparing them a light breakfast that she had just finished up.

"Here you go, babe." She handed him a cup of coffee as he came out of the bathroom brushing his teeth.

He took the cup and sat it down on the table by the couch. Then he picked up his pants to retrieve his phone.

"That thing has been going off all morning. I was going to wake you, but you look so peaceful sleeping, I figured it could wait," she said as she put two plates of food on the table in the kitchen and sat down to eat.

"Hurry, babe, before your food get cold and you have to microwave it."

Mack went back in the bathroom and came back out a few minutes later, picked his coffee up, took a drink, and went and sat down at the table with Kat.

He gave her a kiss. "Good morning, ma. I see yo ass been up for a while."

"Only for a hour or so. I hate sleeping on that couch, so I got up around eight."

He looked at his phone. It was 11 o'clock now. He saw he had several missed calls from Solo, Bo and a few other people, and one from Rob. He checked his voicemail to see if any of them had left a message while he took a bite of toast. Solo left a message saying it was urgent. Bo left one that said, 'Get at me', and then there was one from the boss Rob, letting him know that they needed to meet and go over something, with Rob that could mean anything. He wanted to call his cousin back first to see what was going on, but Rob had left his message at 9 am, over two hours ago and he hated to be kept waiting, so he knew he better call him back first. He dialed his number and on the third ring he picked up.

"Nice of you to return my call so promptly, Travon." Rob always called Mack by his government name.

"Sorry about that, Rob. I had a little too much to drink last night and overslept, that's all." Mack hated explaining himself, but always made an exception when it came to the boss.

"It's ok. Everyone is entitled to sleep in even once in a while, even though I never do myself, as I always say time is money. If I had a choice, I wouldn't sleep at all."

Mack believed him. The man was always calling at odd hours, early in the morning, then late at night. He was probably a vampire or had sold his soul to the devil. That thought made him smile. Kat looked at Mack and wondered what he was smiling about.

"Well, you're up now and that's all that matters. I need you to stop by my house and pick up my Murcielago and drive it to Marina Del Rey. In the glove compartment there is a key to my boat. It's docked at the yacht club. I need you to bring her to me. I'm at the condo in Catalina. You can take the helicopter back. You need to be here by two, is that clear?"

"Yeah, I got it."

"Ok, then I'll see you at two."

Mack knew Rob wanted to discuss some business, but would never talk over the phone. So now he had to go all the way out to Catalina Island and he only had three hours to get there. He knew he better get moving now.

"Have you ever been to Catalina?" he asked Kat while he scarfed down his food.

"No, but I always wanted to go," she said with a big smile, knowing what was coming next.

"Well, today's your lucky day, babe. But we got to hurry, so let's get going," he said as he walked to the room and began to go through the closet to find something to wear.

Kat was right on his heels.

⋏

Forty-five minutes later they pulled up to a Mansion in Bel Air. The street was lined with luxurious homes. The neighborhood was over the top maintained. There were gardeners everywhere to make sure every thing stayed perfect Mack stopped at a ten-foot tall, black gate. He rolled his window down and pushed the talk button on the intercom, a few seconds later, the voice of a lady with a deep Mexican accent came through the speaker.

"Yes, may I help you?"

"Elizabeth, it's me, Travon. I'm here to pick up Mr. Swagner's car."

"Yes, you are late, Travon. I was expecting you a hour ago. The keys are in the car."

A minute later the gate began to slowly swing open, revealing a beautiful house. It had a stone paved circular driveway with a huge water fountain in the middle. Parked in front of the house was a dark blue Lamborghini Murcielago Lp640 Roadster. Mack had driven some of Rob's cars from time to time, but he had just bought the Lambo, so this would be Mack's first time driving it.

"Damn babe, Robert is really balling. This house is off the hook," Kat said as she grabbed her purse and exited out of Mack's Benz.

Kat looked around and was memorized by everything she was taking in. She had never actually stepped foot in a mansion before. Even though they were just inside the gate, it was still an amazing experience for a girl so young. Mack walked to the Lamborghini and pushed the door handle down.

The door slowly swung upwards. Kat was having a bit of trouble, so he ran around and helped her.

"Thank you, babe" she said as he closed the door back down.

Mack got in and pulled off. As they drove down Santa Monica Blvd. trying to make their way to the freeway, Mack kept checking his watch. Traffic was heavy and he did not want to be late. They finally made it to the 405. He quickly made his way to the carpool lane and put his foot on the gas. The car accelerated so fast, it slammed them both back in their seats. When Kat looked over at the speedometer, she saw they were going 135 and still climbing fast. They changed freeways so fast, it felt like they were on a rollercoaster. They were passing cars so fast, it seemed like the other cars were standing still. Before you knew it, the 90 Freeway had run out and they were at the Marina. The car's motor wound down to a purr as they came to a stop at a light.

"Damn, I got to cop me one of these." The car was the fastest thing Mack had ever driven and he loved it.

"I'm just glad we made it here alive, babe," Kat said as she checked her hair and makeup in the mirror, making sure everything was still intact.

"Babe, you know you ok when you with me. I learned how to drive before I walked," he said as he flashed a mouthful of perfectly even teeth.

Kat couldn't help but laugh.

"Whatever, babe. You were driving so fast, I had to close my eyes and just pray."

"I was wondering why you didn't scream when I almost hit that truck," he was saying as they pulled in the parking lot of the yacht club.

The lot was half full with cars and there were rows of boats in all shapes and sizes docked in the water fifty feet in front of them. The look of horror on Kat's face was too much for Mack to bear. He started laughing so hard he could hardly park the car.

"Damn, baby, you should have seen your face. Ha-ha! I was just kidding, ma."

Kat slapped him on his leg.

"That was not funny, babe. You scared me."

"I'm sorry. Come here."

He opened up her door, pulled Kat up into his arms, and gave her a big hug. He checked his watch again.

"Oh shit, babe. We got to hurry up. Come on!"

He grabbed her hand and they quickly walked towards the docks. They came up on a 58-foot speedboat called the Morning Star.

"I hope you don't get seasick, because I'm gone have to take this bitch to the limit once we get out in open water. She goes pretty fast."

"Is it ok for me to look around?"

"Sure."

"My dad's friend has a boat. We always used to go deep sea fishing when I was younger, so no, I don't get seasick," she said as she disappeared below the deck.

The boat was nicely furnished. It had tan leather couches along the walls, a white marble coffee table and thick cream wall-to-wall carpeting, a 40-inch LCD TV on the wall, and a stove and microwave in a small kitchen. She walked into the bedroom. It was decorated in different shades of blues. There was a fish tank built inside one of the walls, a small TV mounted to the dresser, a queen size daybed to the left, and to the right there was a door wide open. Kat could see it was a full bathroom with a glass shower. This was much nicer than her father's friend's, she thought.

Without notice, she was thrown onto the bed as the boat picked up speed.

"I guess we're in open water," she said to herself as she picked up the remote and turned on the TV.

CHAPTER 15

Mack punched in the coordinates on the navigation system and put the boat on autopilot as he picked up his phone and dialed Solo on the boat's satellite phone.

"Yeah, hello?" Solo yelled.

As he answered the phone, Mack could barely hear him over the loud rap music playing in the background.

"Man, turn that bullshit down, dawg. I can barely hear you."

"Hold on a minute." The phone went silent for a second, and then Solo came back on the line after he had put his blunt out and turned off the music in his car.

"Man, nigga, you took long enough to call me back. Where you at?"

"In traffic. What's up?"

Mack never liked to tell people where he was located. He liked to keep them guessing.

"Man, you not going to believe what happened, dawg. This bitch Danielle sent the boys to my spot."

"Who the fuck is Danielle, blood?"

"Danielle is Lil Man's sister, nigga. They were asking all kinds of questions. Shit I knew nothing about, of course."

"Yeah, of course. Look, my nigga, say no more. I got the shit under control. Just text me her address and I'll handle the rest."

"Ok, blood. I hope you take care of this shit, cause I'm not trying go to jail."

Mack took the phone from his ear and looked at it as if it was covered in shit. The comment Solo just made had him feeling he could not be trusted, but he was his closest family member next to Blazz, so he let the shit go.

"Man, just relax, nigga. Ain't nobody going to jail. I said I got everything under control, blood. Just text the fucking number to my phone."

And with that said, he hung the phone up and dialed Bo's number. It rang a few times before he answered.

"What up. Who's this?"

"It's me, T-Mack."

Bo was happy to hear from Mack. He had been waiting on his call all day.

"What's up, blood. I need you to come through with 10 of those things. I got a nigga from the ATL on standby right now. I know you gone give me a good deal."

Mack thought for a moment as he went over things in his head.

"Yeah, I got a great deal for you. You can have that shit for free."

"Nigga, stop playing. That shit is forty-thousand dollars' worth of green, blood."

"Naw, nigga. It's fifty thousand dollars' worth. Plus I know you gone jack the price up sky high on those out-of-towners. But check it out, dawg. I need you to go handle something for me. I got this rat problem I need you to take care of tonight, and when I come outside tomorrow, I will bring you the 10 p's. How's that sound?"

Bo could not believe his ears. He was going to make a shitload of money on this deal. He just hoped it was a one-man job so he would not have to spilt the money with anyone else.

"That shit sound like music to my ears, blood. How many rats we talking about?"

"One female and whoever else is around. I'm going to text you the addresses as soon as I get it, ok?"

"Alright, dawg. I'ma take care of that for you as soon as you slide the info. Then I'll come by the shop tomorrow."

"Good looking, blood," Mack said as he spotted the Island in the distance.

"No problem, nigga. Just hurry up and send the address so I can get started."

Mack hung up the phone and slowed the boat down as he approached the Island.

⚔

Robert Swagner was standing on his balcony hitting golf balls into the ocean, getting ready for a game he had scheduled at 2:30 with group of politicians who had flown in from DC and were at the golf club waiting on his arrival.

The maid walked in. "Mr. Swagner, there's a man by the name Travon at the door for you."

"Bring him to me, please," he yelled over his shoulder.

He continued to practice his game. A few minutes later, Mack appeared in the doorway.

"Nice condo. How many spots you got, anyway?"

Rob hit one more ball into the ocean, then put his club in the case with the others.

"Quite a few. But that's not important. We need to talk business," he said as he sat down on the couch, motioning for Mack to do the same.

"Look, Travon. Word on the street is that you have some loose ends out there. One is running her mouth to the cops and the other is saying he wants you dead."

Rob smiled at the confused look on Mack's face. He knew he was wondering how he always knew every move he made.

"Why the puzzled look? You know I always keep track of my investments. Now, you know I don't mind you making extra money on the side, as long as it does not interfere with what we got going, understood?"

"Yeah, I understand, Rob, and I have things under control, so you can relax."

"Good. Good. That's what I like to hear." He took a thick envelope off the table and passed it to Mack.

"All the information you need for your next job is in there. The mark is some prick on the Los Angeles County Zoning Committee Board. He won't play ball and he is holding up a new development project worth billions. We tried everything, but he just won't get onboard. So he has forced our hand."

Rob stopped speaking as the maid came in and handed him a small wooden box.

"Is there anything else you need, sir?"

"No, that will be all."

He opened the box, took a Cuban cigar out, cut the tip off, placed it in his mouth, then lit it. The maid closed the door behind her as she left the room.

"Like I was saying, he won't play ball, so that's where you come in. It needs to look like an accident. We don't need anymore hold up's on this project."

"What kind of accident do you want him to have?" Mack said as he shoved the envelope in the pocket of his jacket.

"Use your imagination. I'm sure you will think of something. This job is real important, Travon. You will be getting a great deal of money if you handle things right. I trust you will take care of those loose ends we talked about soon."

"I said it's under control, Rob. I always handle my business. Is that all?"

Mack was beginning to get irritated with Rob always in his shit and he could not wait until the day when he answered to no one.

"Yes, that all. I trust you can find your way out. I don't mean to be rude, but I have to get ready for a prior engagement."

"No problem," was all Mack said as he got up and exited the room.

He was going to have to find out who was keeping tabs on him for Rob. He didn't like the fact that his every move was being watched.

Chapter 16

Bo had been sitting in his car for the past two hours watching a small one-story white house. There was a light on in the front room and every once in a while he would see a shadow pass by, so he knew that someone was home. It was ten o'clock at night and the street was quiet except for the old men drinking beer a few houses down. They had been there when he pulled up and he was getting tired of waiting for them to leave, but he did not want to be messy and leave witnesses, so he knew he would just have to be patient. He leaned back in his seat and just listened to his surroundings with his eyes closed. Thirty minutes passed. Then he heard a door slam shut and when he looked up, both men were gone. The light was out in the house, but he could see the light from a TV was still on.

He exited his car and quickly closed the door, making sure he didn't alert anyone. He walked up the driveway and unlatched the wooden gate to the back yard. Once inside, he paused and listened for dogs and anything else that could mean trouble. Once he was satisfied he was alone in the dark yard, he pulled his gloves out and slipped them on. Then he grabbed the screwdriver from his back pocket and began to make his way around the house until he came to a back door. He tried to turn the handle but it was locked. When he came around to the other side of the house, he saw a small window that was slightly cracked open. It was too high to reach so he went back around to the other side of the house and grabbed a big black trashcan and rolled it quietly back to the other side of the house and placed it right below the window. He put the screwdriver back in his pocket and climbed on top of the can, holding onto the wall for balance.

He looked through the small opening in the window and saw that it was a bathroom. The door inside was wide open and he could see a dimly lit hallway. He slowly pushed the window all the way open and pulled himself through head-first, grabbing the towel rack for support and almost dropping his gun as he landed softly on his feet.

"Shit," he mumbled to himself.

He listened to hear if there was any movement going on in the rest of the house. The only noise was coming from the TV in the front, so he quietly made his way up the hallway, checking every room as he passed by. Both of them were empty, so he kept going until he reached the kitchen. The light over the stove was on. He looked around and saw two pots on the counter. He had not eaten in a few hours, so at the smell of food, his stomach began to growl. He peeked under both lids. One pot had fried chicken resting on a bed of paper towels and the other had spaghetti and meatballs. Everything was still warm, but now was not the time to be thinking about food. He walked towards the living room, but paused when he heard a phone ringing in one of the back rooms he had just passed.

"I'll get it, auntie," he heard a female voice say in the next room.

He could hear footsteps coming his way, so he had to think fast. He was sure the rest of the house was empty. Whoever was there was in the front room and one of them would be coming around the corner right about now.

As the girl came through the doorway, she stopped in her tracks. She was so shocked, she couldn't even scream.

Bo calmly whispered her name. "Danielle?"

She did not answer, but he could see the recognition in her eyes. He raised his gun up, placed the barrel between her eyes and pulled the trigger once. The silent pistol barely made a noise as its bullets tore through her skull, forcing her brains out the back of her shattered head. Her lifeless body hit the floor.

"Danielle, are you ok, baby? It sound like you fell or something," the older lady called from the living room.

There was no answer, however. Bo slowly stepped over the corpse, and then entered the living room. The women had her back towards him as she sat in a chair watching an old black-and-white movie.

"Danielle, did you hear me, girl?" she called out behind her.

Bo pointed the gun directly at the back of her head without her having the slightest idea that he was even there. When he pulled the trigger, her face drooped down instantly, her chin resting on her chest as if she were asleep.

Chapter 17

Kat lay on Mack's chest listening to his heartbeat. She could hear the surf pounding against the rocks outside their hotel window. They had decided to spend the night on the Island and go home in the morning. Kat had a wonderful time shopping and eating at the local restaurants. Mack took her horseback riding and once it got dark, they had decided to go have drinks at a bar. They couldn't get in, however, because they were both underage, so they went to their hotel room and ordered a bottle of wine through room service.

"You're quiet babe. What are you thinking about?"

Kat was studying Mack's face. She could tell he was in deep thought. It seemed like something was troubling him.

"Someone's been spying on me for Rob and I think I just figured out who it might be. The shit been on my mind all day."

"Why would Rob need someone to spy on you? I thought you guys were cool."

"Yeah, me too. But the nigga wants to know my every fucking move. I guess he doesn't trust me."

"Why do you need him anyway. You got enough money to do whatever you want. You can be your own boss."

Mack liked the sound of that, but knew it wasn't that simple. Rob would never let him walk away. If he left, his family would be in danger and he would be responsible for whatever happened to them. The only way he could see himself getting out was to gain power over Rob and that seemed impossible.

"Rob's ok. Shit, that nigga keeps money in my pocket and sometimes he can be a lot of fun. If it wasn't for him, shit I'd probably be dead or in prison. But look at us. We in a $300 room drinking hundred dollar bottles of wine in front of a remote control fireplace."

"As long as you happy, babe, I'm happy," Kat said as she took a sip of wine and climbed on top of Mack.

"And if we both happy, that's all that matters." She leaned forward and began to suck on Mack's neck.

"Now you trying to start something," he said as he turned the fireplace up.

He lay back and enjoyed his woman's expert lips.

CHAPTER 18

Bo turned off Adams and headed south on Crenshaw in his CLS 55 Mercedes Benz. His cousin, Bad News, was riding shotgun. They were headed to the shop to meet with Mack.

"Man, why the fuck your car smell like chicken and spaghetti, blood?"

"Because there's chicken and spaghetti in the back seat."

Bad News looked over his shoulder and spotted the pots resting on the floor.

"Man, that shit smell good. Let me get a piece of chicken, nigga?"

Before Bo could answer, Bad News had already opened up the pot, fished out a drumstick and taken a bite.

"This shit is good, blood. I love fried chicken. Even when it's cold."

Bo looked at his cousin eating and wondered if he would still eat the chicken if he knew where it came from.

"Don't get no grease on my seats dawg. I just had this bitch detailed."

He drove into a gas station on Jefferson and Crenshaw and pulled up to a pump. He began to open his door when Bad News tried to stop him.

"Hold up, dawg. Let me run in. I don't think you should get out over here dressed like that."

Bo looked down at his clothes. He had on red Chuck Taylors, jeans and a red T-shirt with a red LA Dodgers cap pulled down over his long braids.

"Man, fuck these niggas."

And with that said, Bo exited the car and walked into the store. Two young guys sitting at the bus stop took notice of him, but remained seated. Bad News reached into his waistband and pulled out his 357 and sat it on his lap. He looked around nervously, making sure they weren't about to be ambushed. Finally he saw Bo coming out of the store with some blunts in his hand. Bo got in the car and passed Bad News the blunts, shaking his head.

"Man, stop looking so damn scary, blood an roll up some of that bullshit, nigga."

"Whatever, nigga. I'm just being safe and you know my shit is fire, nigga. So don't even front."

Bad News pulled out a kush bag and removed a small amount of kush weed and began to break it down.

"I'm gone show you fire, nigga. Wait till you see the shit Mack got for us. We about to be on. I'm going to sell the shit to the ATL niggas and turn around and take my money right back to Mack. He said whatever I spend, he gone front me the same."

"Damn, nigga. I knew Mack was balling, blood, but you telling me when you bring the 50-thousand back to him, he gone front you another 50-thousand dollars worth of kush? Shit, niggas. We on, blood," Bad News said.

Then he hit the blunt. Bo opened the sunroof to let the potent smoke out and thought about all the money he could be making in the very near future. They passed by the Baldwin Hills Mall. People were everywhere standing at bus stops, crossing streets, and walking in and out of different shops. A group of girls waved at Bo and Bad News as they drove by. Bo was too busy thinking about money to notice them, but Bad News rolled down the window and threw his hands up.

"What's up, sexy?"

Bo looked over at his cousin and shook his head. "Nigga, get your dumb ass back in the car before you get us bumped up by one time."

"Man, did you see those bitches? They was bad, blood. We need to go back and holla at them," Bad News said as he rolled his window back up.

Bo looked at him like he had lost his mind. He turned Gucci Mane up. The bass vibrated the rearview mirror as the song "Murder for Fun" played.

A few minutes later they had arrived at the shop. Bo parked in front and they both got out and walked through the front door of the shop. There were ten barber stations. Eight of them were occupied with people getting their haircut. There were about eleven people sitting in the waiting area. Everyone stopped momentarily when the two men entered. Mack peeked his head through the back door and motioned them to come on. Then everyone else went back to what they were doing as the two men disappeared through the doors.

"What up, dawg?" Mack greeted both men with a shake and a pound of the hand.

"What up, Bad News? Yo young ass still a virgin?" Mack teased Bad News because he was the youngest member of their very small circle.

"Whatever, blood. I get pussy all they time. You tripping."

"Is that right? All the time? What that shit smell like then, nigga?"

Bo and Mack broke out laughing, but Bad News didn't see what was so funny. He changed the subject.

"So this is the shit right here?" he said as he grabbed a fluffy brick off the table.

"Yeah that's it. Each brick is a pound. It's all OG kush from Humboldt County. They gonna love that shit in the ATL. Guarantee they come running back."

Bo picked up the bag and tried to smell it, but the bag was vacuum-sealed airtight.

"Yeah, if you open that shit up, you gone have the whole shop high, niggas hair gone be fucked up."

Mack grabbed ten pounds and threw it in a black garbage bag. He handed it to Bo.

"Nice job, blood," was all he said.

He never discussed a murder once it was done. Nothing good could ever come of it and Bo knew that Mack never wanted details. As long as the job got done he was happy.

"No problem, blood. Bad News, pull the car around to the back."

Bo tossed Bad News the keys and watched him walk out the door.

He turned to Mack. "Look, blood. I'm going take this shit to the Atlanta boys. Then I'm going to come back with 50 G's, but I need you to put me on with twenty pounds and I'll pay you later when I dump the shit."

"You got that, but where you gonna dump all that shit?" Mack knew Bo was a dope dealer and had just started fucking with the weed game, so it might take him a while to get rid of twenty pounds of high-grade weed.

"I'm gone take that shit to Atlanta, blood. They paying like eight to twelve thousand a pound, so imagine what I can do with twenty p's, blood. I'm going to make a killing."

Mack liked the sound of those numbers. He had over a hundred pounds and he was getting them for two thousand, so if he could dump them for ten thousand, he would make a great deal of money.

"Shit, at those prices, I want a piece of that action too, nigga."

"No problem, blood. How you want to do it? You gone go with yo boy OT?"

"Naw, this is how we gone do it. You catch a flight out there and get everything ready and when you're ready, I will send you fifty pounds. Twenty-five for me and twenty-five for you. Once you send back the money, I'll send you another fifty and we will keep working it like that."

All Bo could see was dollar signs. He knew this was his chance to move to the next level of the game and he was ready.

"I like the way that sound, blood. We about to blow up for real. Shit, I think I'm gonna fly back there tomorrow. Yeah, that's what's up."

"Take a few homies with you and when you get there I'll have my nigga Forest from Little Rock drop some straps off to you. He will also be able to hook you niggas up with whatever y'all might need."

There was a car blowing its horn in the alley. They both looked up at the camera monitor and saw Bad News at the back gate.

"Ok, nigga. I'll call you when I get out there. Stay up, blood."

Mack and Bo shook hands and gave each other a hug.

"Be safe and don't trust no one," Mack told Bo as he locked the back door.

He looked at his watch and saw that it was two o'clock. Kat wouldn't be out of school for two hours so he decided to hop in his truck and hit the Eastside and go fuck with his homies.

Chapter 19

Leelee, Red and slick were on the side of the house when they heard Mack pull up. The music from the truck shook the ground as he parked in front of the house. They all looked up from the game once they heard the music, but quickly returned to the game once they saw who it was.

"Hit dice," Leelee yelled out as he rolled the dice out after shaking them a few times in his hand.

Six was his point.

"Bet fifty that don't hit," Slick yelled out as he threw fifty more dollars on the ground.

Leelee reached in the pile of money he had between his legs and threw two twenties and a ten on top of the one hundred and fifty already on the ground between the two of them.

"The block," Leelee yelled.

He rolled the dice. When the dice stopped rolling, six was showing again. Leelee quickly scraped all the money up and put it with the rest of his winnings.

"Bet two hundred, blood," Slick yelled as he reached in his pocket and pulled out a big role of hundreds.

He was not happy about Leelee winning his money. He had already lost fifteen hundred dollars to him.

Mack walked up to the group and was greeted with handshakes and pounds.

"What up, big baller. You come to lose some of that cash you got?" Leelee said.

He had a big smile on his face as he counted his winnings.

"Nigga, I don't know why you counting that shit. The game ain't over, blood." Slick wanted action at winning his money back.

"These niggas been at it for hours," Red said to Mack.

He had won a few hundred on side bets, but was getting tired of standing around gambling. He knew Slick and Leelee could go at it for hours, only stopping when someone's pockets were empty.

"Check it out, blood," Mack said.

He waited until he had everyone's attention before he kept going.

"I got some work for y'all. I need you three to go take care of this old dude with me. I got ten G's for each of you, so y'all in or what?"

"Hell yeah, nigga," Red said.

"You know I'm in, nigga." Leelee already had the money spent in his head.

Slick was still thinking. It's not that he was scared; he just liked to think things through before he made a decision.

"Why you need us if it's just one old nigga? Shit, I know you can handle this shit by yourself. What's the catch?"

Mack looked at Slick for a second before answering. Slick was his boy, but sometimes he wished he would go along without asking twenty-one questions first.

"Man, just get in the truck and I'll explain it to you niggas on the way."

Red and Leelee were in the truck before Mack reached the driver's door. Slick got in the front passenger seat last, then looked over at Mack.

"So why you need us?"

Mack wanted to tell him to shut the fuck up and stop thinking so much, but he had too much respect for Slick to talk to him that way, so he just answered his questions.

"Look, the reason I need you niggas is because I don't want it to look like no hit, so Leelee will get you past the alarm on the house, then you three will go in and stack all the dud's valuable stuff up in his garage like you were trying to rob him. Then when he come home, one of you niggas hit him in the head with the bat and get the fuck out of there once you know he is dead. I'm going to be parked at one end of the block watching for the law and Solo ass will be at the other end. When you leave, take his car and dump it a few blocks away. Me and Solo will be right behind you niggas."

Slick was thinking it over as they left the Eastside and got on the freeway headed towards South Pasadena.

"That shit sound easy. You got a bat, gloves and all the tools to get in the house?"

"Man, what the fuck you think?"

Mack was really getting tired of all the questions. He reached to turn up his music when Slick started talking back.

"So when is Solo gonna get there? You should have had him there already so he could be scoping things out."

Mack wanted to scream, 'Shut the fuck up!' Instead, he just took a deep breath and let it out.

He calmly replied, "He's already there. He has been there for three hours already. You know I got shit under control on my end. You just make sure things go down as planned once you niggas get inside."

Slick just shook his head and leaned back in his seat, finally satisfied. Twenty minutes later they were exiting the 110 Freeway on Orange Grove. The neighborhood they were driving through was lined with Victorian style mansions that resembled the White House. They navigated their way through the beautiful homes until they came to the address they were looking for.

"Damn, this old nigga rich as a mutha fucka."

Leelee was looking at the three-story white house. It had four huge pillars that ran from the first story to the second. The windows in the front were big enough to pull a car through and the front lawn seemed as big as a football field. There was no gate around the house and Solo said he couldn't spot any cameras on the house.

"That's Solo parked down there in the white cable van. He's going take y'all back to the hood once everything is done. He has the thirty G's with him, so you niggas will get paid as soon as y'all get in with him."

They all liked the fact that the money was down the street waiting for them.

"Let's get this show on the road. I'm gonna need some wire cutters, a Phillips screwdriver and a flathead screwdriver," Leelee said.

Mack got out of the truck and retrieved the tools from the back, plus a bat and three pairs of gloves. He then got back in and passed everything out.

"Ok I'm going to drop you niggas off in the driveway so people won't see three black dudes walking around in this probably all white neighborhood."

He pulled his truck all the way to the back of the long driveway that ran up the right side of the house. All three men get out and they quickly moved to the back gate. Red checked the gate and it was locked from the side. Slick jumped up and pulled himself over the fence with the speed and stealth of a cat. Within seconds he had unlocked the gate and let the other two in. When the gate closed behind them, Mack began backing out of the driveway so he could go take up his position down the street and keep point. Leelee found the phone lines and unscrewed the top of the box using a Phillips screwdriver. Then he searched for the wires that connected the alarm and cut them with wire cutters while Red watched his back. Slick was looking around the house for the best way in. Once he found what he was looking for, he made his way back to the others.

"There's a sliding door that I can get in easy. You niggas done yet?"

Leelee put the tools back in the bag, then closed the phone box up.

"Yeah, we good. Let's go."

Slick led them to the sliding back door. Then got the flathead screwdriver from Leelee and pushed it in between the glass and the frame. He turned it to the right very slowly and the whole glass door cracked into a light spider web-like pattern but remained together without making the slightest noise.

"You got to teach me that shit," Leelee said as he admired Slick's work.

Slick then pushed a small section of the glass out of the way. He reached in and unlocked the door and slid it open.

Solo sat in the cable van talking on the phone with one of his stripper girlfriends when the line beeped.

"Hold on, little mama I got to take this call." He clicked the line over to see what his cousin wanted. "What up, blood?"

"I just got off the phone with Red and he said they up in that bitch, so we good. We just got to keep a look out for the old dude so we can give them a heads up. He should be here in a hour or two."

"Ok, got it." Solo clicked back over and continued his conversation with the stripper.

"So what's up? I'ma see you tonight or what?"

Slick was in the upstairs master bedroom checking for guns, money or anything valuable while Leelee and Red did most of the work staging the house to look like a burglary. Slick looked in all the drawers and under the bed, but there was nothing worth his time. Then as he was leaving the room, he spotted a dark brown wooden box. He walked over and lifted the lid up. Staring him in the face were six presidential Rolex watches. He quickly took them out of the case and dumped them in his pocket. Then he moved to the next room.

Forty-five minutes had gone by when Mack spotted a silver Lincoln Town Car passing by him. At that same moment, Solo called.

"What's up?" Mack said as he checked the license plates on the car to see if they matched the ones he had stored in his smart phone.

"That's our boy, blood." Solo had already recognized the mark.

"Ok, blood. Good job."

Mack hung up on Solo and quickly dialed Red. The phone rang once, then Red was on the line.

"Yeah?"

"He's pulling up now so be ready, ok?"

"Ok, we on it." Red hung the phone up and called out to the others.

"It's showtime, blood. Let's go."

Leelee stopped what he was doing when he heard Red call and ran to where he was standing in the middle of the living room. At the same time, Slick came running down with the bat in his hand.

"What's cracking? He here?" Slick's adrenalin was pumping and he was ready to take care of business.

"Yeah. Mack said he just pulled up."

Red and Leelee were watching to see how Slick wanted to handle things. He ran to a front window and peeked through the curtains. When he looked outside, he saw a slim white man with silver gray hair in a navy blue suit carrying a black briefcase. The man was coming up the walkway to the front door all by himself. He looked to be in his late fifties.

Slick ran to the door and stood off to the left side. He motioned for the others to get out of sight. He could hear keys jiggling on the other side of the door. He knew the man would be entering the house any second.

He gripped the bat tightly with both hands as he held it up in a batter's stance. He wiped a beam of sweat off his head with his arm. The house was deathly silent. The only sound came from the locks sliding back. Then the door slowly swung open and the unsuspecting man stepped through.

Slick kicked the door closed and with one swift swing, the bat came crashing down on the guy's head. The man took two steps, hit the wall and slid down to the floor, landing in a sitting position. His eyes were still open as he stared straight into nothingness.

Slick raised the bat up high, and then brought it down hard, striking the man once more in the same spot. Blood flew against the wall and covered the man's face. A large pool of blood formed on the floor.

Leelee and Red were now standing behind Slick with shocked looks on their faces. They had seen plenty of guys get shot, but they had never witnessed anything like this before. Slick looked over his shoulder and let out a little laugh when he saw their expressions.

"Let's go," was all that he said as he picked up the car keys and walked out the door.

Chapter 20

Five months had passed and things were going great. Mack was making all the right moves. He and Bo were moving fifty pounds of kush a month at ten thousand apiece in Atlanta. Mack's cut was 350 thousand. He was making so much money that he ran out of room in the safe in his storage unit, so he began putting it in boxes in the spare bedroom of his condo. His barbershops were also doing well. In addition to that, he had just purchased a car lot that specialized in high-end cars. It was located on Fairfax in West LA. Kat was still going to school full time and had moved in with Mack in his Westchester condo.

"Damn, babe. My bro about to come home. I can't wait till his ass get out next week," Mack said to her as he climbed out of bed.

He walked in the living room and turned on the TV to the morning news. Kat came in after him. She walked to the fish tank and began to feed them the dry fish food that was kept inside of the stand.

"Yeah, I think we should throw him a big party. I could invite some of my friends from school. He might get lucky and get some with his young ass." She was laughing as she put the rest of the fish food up and went and sat next to Mack on the couch.

"He's definitely getting lucky if you invite those ho's."

"Whatever, boy. My friends aren't ho's. They just having fun while they're still young."

"Is that what they call it now? Well, where I'm from, if you sleeping with multiple niggas, you a ho."

Kat didn't feel like arguing about her friends, so she decided to get the subject back on track.

"If you want, I can plan the party for you, babe. I need something to keep me busy, anyways."

"Don't I keep you busy, ma?"

Mack had a smirk on his face. He reached over and started tickling Kat.

"Stop, babe," she yelled, between laughs.

"You know yo ass ain't never home," she said once she stopped laughing. "Plus I like doing things like that anyway. So just give me a budget and I will get started today."

"Well, just use the black card and don't go to crazy, ok?"

He shot her a serious look. He knew Kat would burn the card out if he let her, but he also knew she would do a great job with the party.

"Don't worry, babe. Just leave everything to me. You don't got to do nothing but show up looking good."

Kat was excited. She couldn't wait to get started. She grabbed her laptop off the floor and let all her and Mack's friends on Facebook know about the party.

◢

Across town, Solo sat in Starbucks watching the two detectives sit in their car. They had been following him for two days. He told Mack about it, but he said not to worry, that they were just trying anything because they had nothing on him. That was easy for him to say, Solo thought to himself. He wasn't the one they were following.

Solo thought he had seen the last of them when Mack took care of the girl, but here they were five months later, following him around like he was Gotti or someone. The shit had him all fucked up in the head. Solo had completely changed his routine up. He hadn't been home in days. He did not want them to know where his new house was. He had moved from his grandmother's house in South Central a few months ago and bought himself a three-bedroom condo in downtown LA, right down the street from the Staples Center. He had not even told Mack about it yet. He was tired of this cat and mouse game and was ready to go home, so he had come up with a plan.

"Yeah, call me when you get here and hurry up."

A few minutes later, he saw a taxicab pull up. Then his phone rang.

"Hello? Yeah, that's you. Well, pull on the other side. My wife's having someone follow me and they're parked over there, so I can't come out that way. Ok, bye."

He hung up the phone and watched the taxi turn around and drive back the other way. Seconds later, it appeared on the other side. Solo got up and walked to the front counter. He asked the young white girl standing on the other side to get the manager.

"The manager's on his lunch break. He should be right back, though," she said with a big cheerful smile.

Solo pulled out a hundred dollar bill and placed it on the counter.

"I'm sorry, sir. We can't change that without the manager's authorization."

"Look, there is someone following me and I need to get out of here now. You can have that if you just let me out the back door."

The girl looked at the money and then back to Solo. She wanted to take the money, but Solo's 6' 300-pound tattooed body was a little frightening. He studied her face and could tell what she was probably thinking. He put another hundred-dollar bill on the counter.

"Look, baby girl, I really need you to make a decision before my taxi leaves."

She looked at the money, then scooped it up and put it in her pocket.

"Come on. Hurry up before my manager gets back."

She led him through the kitchen and opened up the back door. When he stepped outside, she quickly closed it shut. He could see the back of the taxi a few feet away. He quickly made his way to it, looking around to make sure that the coast was clear. When he hopped in and slammed the door, the cab driver jumped in his seat.

"Shit, man you scared the fuck out of me!" The driver looked like he could have been a hippie or a biker.

"Look, get me downtown fast."

He tossed two hundred dollar bills at the driver, then lay all the way down across the back seat. The driver took one look at the money and stepped on the gas.

CHAPTER 21

Mack was in the apartment above his barbershop weighing out the shipment of kush that had just came in from Humboldt County. He had called Slick in to help him get it prepared to be sent to Bo in Atlanta. Usually his right hand man Solo would be there to help, but Mack had not seen him in a week. He had talked to him several times over the phone, however, and it sounded like his cousin was losing his mind. He had locked himself up somewhere and refused to let anyone know where he was at. He claimed the cops were staked out in front of his grandmother's house and he was afraid that they were after him. For what, he didn't know. But he wasn't trying to find out.

"Yeah, blood. That nigga Solo been tripping lately. He acting paranoid and shit. I think I'm ah send him to Atlanta with Bo so he can chill out," Mack said to Slick as he weighed out another ten pounds and put them on the floor with the rest of the weed.

"Is the nigga coming to Blazz's party tonight?"

"Shit, I don't know what that nigga doing, but he starting to get on my nerves. The boy acting like a bitch."

"Shit, if I was you, blood, I would just take his ass out before the nigga do something stupid. The nigga know way too much."

"Blood, I ain't about to kill my family, nigga. You tripping. Plus Solo a stand up nigga. I don't think the nigga would snitch... Naw, he wouldn't go out like that," Mack replied.

He got up off the couch and went to the bar to fix himself a shot of Patron. He knew Slick was right. If it was anyone else, he would have had them killed, but he just couldn't make the call on Solo. He loved him, and until now, trusted him with his life. The only person on Earth he was closer to was his brother, Blazz.

"Well, you better keep a closer eye on him. If you won't, I will go check on his ass for you."

Slick was ready to get rid of Solo because he thought he was next in line to take his place. Plus he loved to kill -- even if it was one of his own people.

"I don't even know where the nigga is, but if he show up tonight, I'm going to have a talk with him and let him know he got to go chill in the ATL for a minute. Let the cops get off his ass."

Mack raised the glass to his mouth and emptied it in one swallow. He then refilled it and carried it into the bedroom with him. He checked out the outfit Kat bought for him to wear to Blazz's party tonight. There were some all-white Louie Vuitton sneakers at the foot of the bed and a white Louie Vuitton belt, some light blue Seven jeans, an all-white Versace long-sleeved, button-down and a white T-shirt. Hanging on the door was his white and gray chinchilla boomer style jacket.

He took a quick shower and changed into his outfit. Then he went to the safe that was behind one of the paintings on the wall and retrieved his diamond chain, three-karat earrings and Breitling watch with the diamond face. When he stepped back into the living room, Slick was just finishing packing up the last box of kush.

"Damn, blood. You trying to shit on everyone, nigga?" Slick blurted out when he saw Mack.

"I'm just doing me, blood! You done yet?" Mack replied as he looked at his watch.

It was ten o'clock at night and Kat had called several times from the club asking where he was. Blazz had already arrived. He had gotten out earlier that day, but Mack still hadn't seen him yet.

"Yeah, I just got done," Slick replied. "Everything is ready to be shipped out on Monday."

"Let's roll out then," Mack said.

He grabbed his keys and headed for the door. Slick was right behind him.

"I know you taking the Benz dressed like that, so let me ride with you, blood. I don't feel like driving the Camaro."

"You can ride with me, but I'm leaving the Benz here. I got something else in the back I just bought."

When Slick stepped outside, he couldn't believe his eyes. Parked next to Mack's CLS55 Benz was an all-white Rolls Royce convertible Ghost 26" three-piece rims with brushed silver lips.

"Nigga, we gone kill the game when we pull up in this bitch. You a fool for this one, blood."

Slick was excited and couldn't wait to get in. He knew all eyes would be on them when they pulled up in front of the party.

⚔

Thirty minutes later across town in Hollywood, Club Mixer was jumping. It was a tri-level club. The top floor was VIP and reserved for Blazz's party. It had a balcony looking down onto Sunset Blvd. There were people walking up and down Sunset going from club to club. There was a line of people going around the block waiting to get into Club Mixer.

When Mack and Slick pulled up and stopped in front, everyone in line stopped what they were doing. When the valet opened up their doors and Mack got out, all eyes were on the young millionaire. The girls in line were half-naked and were trying their best to get his attention, but he was busy looking at the large banners that hung from the walls of the club with his brother's picture and name on them welcoming him home.

'Blazz' was even written across the red carpet that led from the street curb all the way to the club doors.

"Damn! How much all this shit cost, nigga?" Slick asked.

Mack just shrugged his shoulders. He had no idea what Kat had spent.

"We here for Blazz's party," Mack told a large Samoan in black pants and a T-shirt that barely fit.

He handed him their ID's. The man checked the list and quickly found their names. He called over an escort.

"They are here for the party. Take them up," he told another Samoan man that was also large, but not as big.

The first Samoan lifted up the velvet rope and let them onto the red carpet. Mack tried to hand him some money, but he shook his head and refused it.

Blazz's guests don't have to pay. Everything is paid for already. Have a nice time."

He turned around and stopped two girls who were trying to make their way past the ropes. Mack and Slick followed the bouncer into the club. As soon as they entered, the music almost overwhelmed them. It was so loud, the bouncer had to signal with his hands when he wanted to communicate with them.

There were people dancing on a very large dance floor and every table was filled with more people who had enough money to order bottle service. The bar was packed with sexy ladies and young playas trying to order drinks. The stage lights were going crazy. The bouncer led them to the elevator. Once they got on and the doors closed, it was much quieter and you could barely hear the music.

"Damn, blood. This shit is cracking. I'm trying to leave with at least two of these bitches," Slick announced to no one in particular. The elevator stopped on the third floor and then the last floor. The doors opened up and once again the music hit them in the face. The bouncer handed Mack and Stranger two VIP wristbands and got back on the elevator. The doors began to close. There were about a hundred people in the VIP area. Mack knew almost all of them. Unlike downstairs, you could move around freely without bumping into anyone. Some people were dancing on a small dance floor, but most were sitting around drinking. Mack looked around and finally spotted Kat and his baby brother sitting in a booth with Bo, Red, Leelee, Bad News, Solo and five of Kat's girlfriends from school. They were all drinking and having a great time. As soon as Blazz saw Mack and Slick walking towards them, he jumped up and ran to meet his big brother.

"T-Mack! What up, big bro?" he yelled with his arms stretched out ready to be embraced.

Mack grabbed him and put him in a bear hug. Even though Blazz was only gone for six months, it seemed like much longer.

"Man, I missed you, little nigga."

"Shit, I missed you too, bro."

Blazz was happy to be home and hoped Mack saw him as a man now that he had done some time and was turning eighteen next week.

"Happy early B-Day, blood. This party is off the hook, huh?"

"Hell yeah. I never expected nothing like this. I feel like the prince of LA, dawg."

Blazz could tell Mack had stepped his game up to the next level and couldn't wait to get put on. They had already talked about Blazz working for Mack since he fucked his football career up and he hoped Mack hadn't changed his mind.

"What's up, babe? You like how I put this party together? Told you I was going to have shit right," Kat said as she walked up to Mack and gave him a hug.

He kissed her and took a good look at her. She had on a pink and baby blue Channel baby doll dress that had a low V-cut in front, showing plenty of cleavage. The bottom stopped way above her knees with some matching high heels. Her hair was mostly pinned up with a few curls hanging down in the front. He knew he had the finest chick in the club.

"Damn, ma. You out did yourself" Mack seed as they all walked back to their booth.

There were bottles of Patron, Moet, Cristal, Belvedere and Hennessey on the table sitting in buckets of ice. Mack shook hands with his crew and sat next to Solo. Before he could bring up the situation, however, the elevator doors opened up and out came Geno dressed in a tailored suit. He spotted Mack and began to make his way towards him. Mack hardly ever saw Geno anymore, ever since he moved to New York last year to help his father out. He hardly was in LA, so this was a nice surprise.

"What up, my man?" Geno said as he and Mack embraced.

"Long time no see. You came out for my bro's B-Day?" Mack asked, still surprised that he was actually there.

"I wish I could say yes, but I'm here on important business. Let's go somewhere and talk. We can have a few drinks together and catch up on things."

Mack hoped nothing was wrong, but he knew it was important for Geno to come to Blazz's party and talk business. They walked to the balcony and found an empty table and sat down. The air outside was filled with smoke. The other two tables had some people Mack didn't recognize sitting around smoking what smelled like very good weed.

"Is everything ok?" Geno pulled out a small envelope and passed it to Mack.

He opened it up and looked inside. There was a photo of a man, plus a slip of paper with the address and name of a strip club, and some other information.

"Yeah, everything is good. We just need a job done. The guy right there is an informant for the Feds. He belongs to Wild Style, an outlaw biker gang. They would take care of him themselves, but they feel it would be better handled from an outside source. He supposed to be leaving town tomorrow, so Rob wants this taken care of in the morning. We had someone else on the job, but he got locked up last night and has a parole hold, so we can't bail him out. So I hope you can handle it."

The shit was last minute notice in a real way, but Mack knew he couldn't say no, so there was no reason to complain.

"Yeah man, you know I got you. Consider it done."

"That's what I wanted to hear," Geno said, shaking Mack's hand while he patted him on the shoulder.

Then they both got up and went back to the party. Mack knew he would need some help. He would usually take Bo or Solo, but Bo was catching a flight back to Atlanta in the morning and he was trying to send Solo with him. He thought about using Slick, but then he saw Blazz on the dance floor dancing with two of Kat's friends. His brother had gotten a lot bigger over the last six months and was beginning to look like a man. Mack felt this might be the right chance for Blazz to prove himself. Mack sat next to Kat, then called Leelee over.

"What up, blood? This party is cracking," Leelee said as he sat down next to Mack.

He was drinking straight from a bottle of Cristal.

"Yeah, I'm glad you having a good time, but I need you to get on the phone and have one of your people put a G-ride near this address." Mack passed Leelee a small folded up piece of paper.

"Ok, I'm ah get right on it."

Leelee took the paper, opened it up and pulled out his phone. He began to text his boy Crook, a Mexican car thief that kept stolen cars parked up and down the street that he lived on.

"Let's dance, babe," Kat whined.

She wanted some attention from Mack. She was tired of all the business taking up Mack's time. She wanted to party with her man.

"One second, babe. Let me holla at my cousin real fast."

"Ok, babe. But hurry up. I'm going to go tell the DJ to play your song," she explained.

She got up and walked towards the DJ booth, Mack raised up and sat by his cousin. Solo was drinking heavily and Mack could tell he was already drunk.

"What's up, baby boy. It looks like you might need to slow down, dawg."

Solo looked at Mack and laughed.

"I'm good, dawg. I just been stuck in the house so I'm trying to cut loose tonight. I pooped three X pills and I'm on one."

Solo had a crazy look in his eyes and Mack knew he would be wasting his time trying to have an intelligent conversation with him right now. He decided to just wait for a better time. Kat had returned and she gave Mack a look that said, 'You better be ready.' At that same moment, the DJ stopped the music and made an announcement.

"I want all the bad chicks and all the ballers to get on the dance floor and shake something or break something for the man who's responsible for this banging event. Give it up for T-Mack, everyone! This one is for him!"

Everyone got up and began to crowd onto the dance floor as the DJ put on an old Lil' Wayne song. He cranked up the volume.

I'm a young money millionaire...

Mack got up and grabbed Kat and pulled her to the dance floor. They began to dance and sing along with the song. Everyone was having a great time. Mack and his crew partied like there was no tomorrow. Blazz and Slick were talking to three of Kat's home girls and before you knew it, they had already disappeared. Mack was happy to see his brother free again and having fun. Him and Kat danced to a couple more songs and when they finally sat down, Blazz and Slick were still missing, so he decided to give them a call. He dialed Blazz's number first. It rang a few times, then a girl answered it and she sounded tipsy.

"Hello?" she yelled through the phone between giggles.

"Who this and were my brother at?"

Mack wanted to know who was answering his brother's phone. The nigga just got out of jail so he knew he did not have a girl.

"He's busy eating my pussy right now and his dick is in my girl's mouth, so can you call back."

Mack couldn't believe his ears. His little bro was getting his freak on with two chicks on his first day out. He just hoped they were bad.

Blazz snatched the phone from the girl. "Hello? Who is this?"

"It's me, Mack. Little nigga, since when you start eating pussy?"

"Whatever, bro. Me and Slick in the stretch hummer with three of Kat's college friends and it's going down."

"Which three y'all got?"

"The one white girl with the blond hair and big ass titties... The tall black girl with the big ass... And the Asian bitch."

"Damn, little nigga. Y'all doing y'all thang. But check it out. I got a job in the morning and I'm taking you with me. So don't get too fucked up."

"Nigga, is you serious?"

Blazz couldn't believe his ears. He was finally going to get his chance to show Mack he was ready.

"Yeah, blood. But if you not ready in the morning, I'm ah know you was not serious. And ain't no second chances."

"You don't got to worry about me. I'm on my way to the hotel off of Rosecrans. Just come get me in the morning. I'll be ready."

"Alright, little nigga. Make sure you wear a rubber," Mack blurted as he hung up the phone laughing.

"What's so funny, babe?" Kat asked.

She had been listing to Mack's conversation, but couldn't put the whole thing together.

"Nothing. Just Blazz young ass is growing up."

"I think you not telling me something, but whatever, babe. I'm ready to go home so I can show you what I got under my dress," Kat replied with a wicked grin.

"Is that right, babe? Well, Blazz already left, plus I got to work in the morning. So let's go see what you got for me," he said with a sly look on his face.

As they got up to leave, Mack noticed most of his crew were still there, even Geno, who was at a table with three beautiful black woman. The only ones who were missing were Blazz, Slick and his cousin Solo. He knew Slick was with his brother, but Solo had disappeared again. He was really beginning to worry about him. He told himself that he would talk to him tomorrow and put him on a plane headed for Atlanta. He would make him stay there until things cooled off.

Chapter 22

Solo was in the club parking lot sitting in his Dodge Viper doing his lines of coke off the thighs of a fine Mexican girl he had just met. She had her mini skirt hiked so far up you could see her panties.

"Give me some, papee," she begged Solo.

He took some more coke out of the bag and made a thick line on his big forearm. It went from his elbow to his wrist. When the girl saw how big the line was, she began to get excited and lick her sexy, full lips.

"That's all for me, papee?"

"Shit, if you can handle it, go ahead ma."

She quickly ducked her head down and began to sniff the coke off his body. She finished the whole line, stopping only once.

"Damn, bitch. You a pro."

The girl just laughed, then reached over and began to unzip his pants.

"Let me thank you, papee. East LA style."

Solo turned on the car and they could feel the rumble from the V10 through both their bodies.

"Damn, that shit feels good. All that vibration when you rev the gas is making my pussy wet."

Solo pushed her head down back in his lap and turned the music on as he peeled out of the parking lot. UGK was playing loud as he sped up Sunset, running several lights. He quickly turned on the 101 Freeway, doing 100 mph. They were both so high, they didn't even notice the highway patrol car behind them flashing its lights. Solo was pushing the sports car to its limit. It barely stayed on the freeway. When he went around a curve at 125mph and then quickly accelerated to 175, the highway patrol car could not keep up and called for air support. The wind had blown the bag of coke open and it was all over the place. The back of the girl's head and Solo's face were covered in it. She was still giving him head and was so zoned out that she hadn't noticed a thing. When Solo saw all the coke on the back of her head, he bent down and started sniffing it off while he blindly steered the speeding car. When she felt him behind her, she lifted her head up and they began kissing like old lovers. They were both so out of it, they hadn't noticed the car leave the freeway heading straight for the center divider at 185 mph. When it made contact, the impact threw the car so high in the air, it appeared like a small plane had taken flight. When it landed, the car rolled the length of three football fields before it came to a complete stop upside down. It all happened so fast, neither passenger ever realized what happened.

When the highway patrol car finally arrived and saw the wreckage, they immediately stopped all traffic and radioed for an ambulance. When the medics arrived on the scene, Solo was still unconscious, hanging upside down. They had to use the Jaws of Life to free him. One of the firefighters noticed a single red high heel shoe on the pavement and a purse hanging from the door they had just cut off.

"I think there was someone in here with him. We need to search the freeway from the beginning of the accident all the way to this point and fast. They might still be alive," the firefighter ordered the rest of the crew.

He then took off running to alert the highway patrol officers that were holding traffic back.

CHAPTER 23

Just as Kat was about to dial Mack's phone for the twentieth time, she heard keys jiggling on the other side of the door. It swung open and Mack walked in all nonchalant with Blazz right behind him, carrying a big black bag.

"What's up, ma? You look like you saw a ghost or something," he joked.

He kissed her on the cheek and sat down, taking took the bag from Blazz who sat right next to him.

"Why you wasn't answering your phone, boy? I been calling you for like twenty minutes!" she shrieked with an angry expression on her face.

She had her arms folded over her chest, standing right in front of Mack.

"Calm down, babe. I had my music up loud and my phone was in my center console, that's all. You thought something happened to daddy?" he added with a big smile on his face.

But Kat didn't see a damn thing funny.

"Ain't noting funny, babe. I was worried about both of you," she whined as she sat on his lap and gave him a kiss.

Blazz stared at both of them impatiently. He was ready to count the money, see how many pills they had come up on and find out what his cut would be.

"Man, y'all got all day for that lovey dovey stuff. Let's count this money, bro," he pleaded.

He began to dump everything out of the bag onto the coffee table.

"Babe, can you get the money counter and the big scale for me?" Mack asked, slapping Kat on the ass as she got up.

"Don't start nothing you can't finish while your little brother around," she replied with a playful wink as she disappeared into the bedroom.

"Nigga, why you got boxes all in the living room? Y'all moving?" Blazz asked, frowning at all the clutter.

Mack looked around at all the brown boxes filled with money. They were stacked up in every empty space he could find in his living room now that the spare bedroom was filled to capacity. He was making so much money he was running out of room to stash it. He knew he was going to have to address the problem soon.

"Don't worry about all that," he ordered.

"Let's just count this lot," he added when he saw Kat walk back in.

She sat both objects on the coffee table and plugged them up. Mack grabbed a stack of hundreds, and then fed them through the machine.

"This shit ain't gonna take but a minute," Mack said as he rubberbanded the first thousand dollars that came through. It took them fifteen minutes to count the money and weigh the pills. Blazz couldn't believe how much money they had made in a matter of a few minutes. He couldn't hardly wait to find out how much was his. Mack, on the other hand, was hardly impressed with what lay on the table on front of them.

"Check it out, little nigga. It's seventy-five thousand in cash and eighty thousand in pills wholesale and the shit all yours. How you feel about that?" Mack asked, already knowing the answer to his own question.

Blazz was speechless. He had already done the math in his head. He had been broke less than an hour ago and now there was one hundred and fifty thousand dollars in cash and drugs in front of him and it was all his. He had no idea how to respond.

"Thhh... Thhh... Thanks," was all he could get out.

Mack and Kat both broke out laughing. They could tell Blazz was in shock at his newly found fortune.

"Thhh... Thhh... Thanks," Mack repeated, making fun of his brother.

He picked up his phone and dialed Geno's number. Geno answered on the first ring.

"Hey, if it ain't my main man, T-Mack. How's it going, bro?" Mack walked into his bedroom so he could talk in private.

"It's going great, G. I hope you had yourself a good time last night."

"Hell yeah, man. You sure know how to throw a party."

"Well, I can't take the credit for that. You got to thank my girl, but the party I threw this morning, that was all me. I just need some help with the bill," Mack said talking in code, letting Geno know that he had done the job and was ready to get paid.

"Man, I wish I could have been there, but I was a little hung over from last night. But I got some extra money too, if it will help you out. Just tell me where you want me to drop it off at," Geno replied back in code.

Mack had already decided it would be best not to bring any more cash to the condo, so he gave Geno the address to his car dealership.

"Just take it to the manager. He know where to put it. And thanks."

"No problem. Consider it done already," Geno replied before hanging up.

Mack then dialed Solo's number, but it went straight to voicemail.

"Damn, this nigga don't ever answer his phone anymore," he blurted out as he dialed the number to his dealership to let the manager know to be on the lookout for Geno.

CHAPTER 24

The next day across town at USC Medical, Solo strained to open his eyes. The bright light in the hospital room was blinding him and it took a few moments for his eyes to adjust. Once they did, he noticed the white cast on his left forearm. His whole body ached with pain, but it seemed nothing else was wrong.

"So you finally decided to wake up, huh?"

A beautiful lady sat in a chair in the corner of the room. He hadn't realized she was even there at first. He couldn't recognize who she was until he tried to move his right hand and heard the distinct sound of metal on metal. He looked down at his wrist and saw he was handcuffed to the bed. He realized who she was.

"Detective Vicenta. Or can I still call you Samantha?"

She got up and stood next to the bed.

"I'm afraid this is not a friendly visit, Mr. Thomas. So 'Detective' will do just fine," she replied as she sat her sexy petite 5'6" frame on the edge of the bed.

She looked him up and down while she shook her head back and forth.

"What's the matter, Detective? You see something you don't like?" Solo asked.

He didn't like the smirk she wore on her face. It made him feel as if she knew something she was keeping to herself.

"I'm just amazed that you're still alive after that car accident. I mean, gosh, your car was totally wreck and all you got is a couple of bruises and a broken arm," she answered, still shaking her head.

"Car accident? What car accident? Is that why I'm in here? Shit, when I saw you I thought LAPD had just beat my ass real bad and I lost consciousness or something," he said being totally serious.

"You mean you don't remember the high-speed chase and then crashing your car into a center divider and rolling your vehicle over three hundred feet, killing your passenger in the process?" she asked.

She threw the picture of the dead girl on the bed. Solo couldn't believe what she had just told him. When he looked at the girl's body, he almost threw up. She was torn apart. Her whole face had been scraped off and she was cut in half at the waist.

"What are you talking about? I don't remember none of this. This shit can't be happening!" he yelled out.

He tried to get up, but she quickly put her hands on his chest and pushed him back down.

"Calm down right now," she ordered.

"Now look, Michael. You got yourself in some deep shit. You were covered in coke and had some X pills in your pocket, not to mention the alcohol level in your blood was three times the legal limit. With all that and how fast you were driving, shit I won't have no problem charging you with first degree murder," she explained.

She looked him in the eye to make sure it was sinking in.

"What the fuck? I didn't kill no one. I don't even remember this shit and I don't even know who that girl is," he pleaded.

But he knew he was fucked. Once a jury saw all the drugs and drinking that he had done -- not to mention he was a big, tall, tatted up black man and a gang member -- he knew he didn't have a chance in hell.

"But today is your lucky day, big boy," she announced as she patted him on the leg.

"We have been watching you guys for a long time and we know all about that son of a bitch Robert Swagner and his group of thugs he has running around terrorizing the city," she blurted out.

She got off the bed as two men entered the room.

"Like I said, we know about at least twenty-one murders, briberies and extortions that have taken place over the last few years that we have been watching you guys."

Solo couldn't believe the mess he was in. He knew life as he had known it was over.

"So how is this my lucky day?" he said, hoping for some light at the end of a very dark tunnel.

"Well, we been trying to get close to the man for years, but no one in his crew has slipped up -- that is, until now," she explained with a big smile.

"This is Jim Newman from the FBI. He's the head of a joint task force that's dedicated to taking down corrupt politicians and city officials."

A young, thin, blond man dressed in gray slacks and a blue shirt with a bulletproof vest on over it nodded his head at Solo. Solo just looked at him, then back to Samantha.

"And this is the DA handling the case against Mr. Swagner and your crew."

"How are you doing, Mr. Thomas?" a black guy wearing glasses who looked to be in his forties said, extending his hand out.

Solo stared at it, then looked back at Samantha.

"Look, Michael. This is it, plain and simple. You can either cooperate with us and be a free man -- you won't spend a day in jail -- or you can go down for the girl you killed last night and never see the streets again. Oh and whenever we do take Swagner down -- which we will, with or without your help -- you will be charged along with the rest of your friends. The choice is yours," Samantha explained as she went to go stand with her two coworkers.

Solo took a long look at all three of them, then closed his eyes, wishing he could go back to sleep and never wake up again.

Chapter 25

Six thousand miles away in Atlanta, Georgia, Bo had just returned to the house after mailing Mack's money back to California. The neighborhood he and his crew had set up in was very affluent. There were only two and three-story brick and stone style mansions for miles. And almost everyone drove high-end vehicles. But when Bo pulled up, he had noticed several cars that stood out like sore thumbs.

"Nigga, have y'all been outside today?" he asked as he entered the very large living room.

Bad News, Baby Monster, Take Off, and Punch were all crowded around the seventy-inch flat screen playing Call of Duty on PlayStation. None of them heard a word he said. Bo ran over and turned the TV off, then dropped the remote down on the hard marble floor. All four young men turned around and stared at him like he had lost his mind, but no one was stupid enough to say a word.

"I said, have you little niggas been out the house while I was gone?"

"Naw, blood. We been right here the whole time," Bad News answered, wondering what had crawled up his big homie's ass.

"Look blood, I think they about to raid the spot. I saw like ten unmarked cars that I never seen around here before."

Bo was pacing back and forth, trying to figure out his next move while everyone else just stared at him like he was tripping.

"Nigga, whatever you been smoking, let me hit that shit," Baby Monster blurted.

The second the words left his mouth, he knew he had fucked up. Everyone was now staring at anything suspicious or out of place.

"Get all the straps and put them in the back yard," Bo ordered.

Baby Monster headed out the front door while the others ran up the stairs. He couldn't believe how slow they were moving to retrieve the two AK 47's and a number of handguns they had acquired through Mack's homeboy Frost when they first arrived in Atlanta.

Bo ran to one of the back bedrooms downstairs where they kept all the weed and money to make sure it was empty. He only kept ten pounds of kush at a time in the house and the rest was kept at a stash house that only he knew the location of. He saw Punch, Take Off and Bad News run by carrying all the weapons, heading for the back door.

"Put them in the rental car," Bo ordered.

He ran towards the living room. When he got there, Baby Monster was coming through the front door.

"Blood, they coming right now!" he yelled between breaths.

Baby Monster had been running nonstop all the way back to the house. Punch, Bad News and Take Off ran back in.

There was a big knock on the front door.

"This is the Atlanta Police Department. Open up!"

Everyone was waiting for Bo. They had no idea what to do next. Bo knew there was no use in trying to run. He laid down on the cold marble floor and put his hands on top of his head. Punch did the same and the other three-followed suit.

A second later, the front door was busted down and an army of cops came running in with bulletproof vests on and guns drawn.

"Freeze! Get the fuck on the ground! Atlanta PD! Don't move! Get down! If you move your fuckin' hands, you're gonna get your head blown off."

CHAPTER 26

Back in Los Angeles, T-Mack put the phone down on the bar and picked the blunt up. He took a long, hard drag, inhaling the smoke into his lungs while he tied to figure out why no one was answering his calls. As he exhaled, he tried Rob's line again. This time a woman's voice came on over the line.

"The number you are calling is no longer in service."

"What the fuck is going on?" he said.

He hung up the phone, cutting off the recording. He had been trying to reach Solo for the last couple of days, but he was getting used to him not answering. Now he had lost contact with Bo, and now Rob's phone was disconnected. Things weren't adding up and he had a bad feeling something big was about to go down. He picked the phone back up and called Blazz.

"What up, big bro?"

Blazz was in a great mood. He had bought himself a platinum Range Rover from Mack's car lot and you couldn't pay him to stay out of it. He was running around LA selling his ecstasy pills left and right.

"Listen up. I need you to go rent a U-Haul truck. The biggest one they got. Then meet me at my condo ASAP," he ordered.

"Damn, nigga. I'm kind of busy right now."

"Man, just do the shit right now, nigga. I don't have time to explain, but it's important," he yelled.

He hung up without waiting for an answer. Then he called Kat.

"Hey, babe. I can't talk. I'm in class right now," she whispered through the phone.

"I'm sorry, ma, but when you get out of school, I'm going to need you to do me a favor, ok? So come straight home," he explained.

"Ok. I get out in twenty minutes and I'll be on my way. Is everything ok? You sound upset," she replied.

"Yeah, I'll explain everything when I see you. I love you."

"I love you too, babe. Bye."

Mack ran downstairs and opened the back door to his shop. He got in his Escalade truck and backed it all the way to the door. He began filling the back up with the hundred pounds of weed that had just came in from Humboldt County. When he was done, he ran to the front and called his head barber Will over. Willie was a Mexican, but had hung out with blacks his whole life and could cut hair better than any barber in the shop.

"What up, Mack. Why you all sweaty, dawg? You been upstairs fucking again, huh?" Will inquired with a wide grin on his face.

Mack was too busy thinking. He didn't even hear what Will had said.

"Look, here is five hundred dollars."

Mack shoved a roll of money in Will's hand. Before he could ask what it was for, Mack continued talking.

"I need you to take my car to 310 Customs and tell the owner I need to leave it there for a while. He knows the truck when he sees it. He's the one who did all the work on it and sold me the rims."

"Ok, but how am I supposed to get back?" Will asked as he stuffed the money in his front pocket and took his barber apron off.

"Call a cab, nigga," Mack yelled as he jumped in his CLS 550 and pushed one of the buttons on his sun visor.

The tall, black metal gate began to open. Mack was flying up Crenshaw headed home. He was so deep in thought he hardly noticed his surroundings. He thought he might be overreacting, but he was not taking any chances. He rather be safe than sorry. His gut was telling him something was wrong and he was not about to ignore it. He decided to shut down all illegal operations until he at least got in contact with Rob and Bo.

When he turned right on Manchester, his phone began to ring. He snatched it off the seat and checked the caller ID. It was an Atlanta area code.

"Damn, let this be Bo," he thought.

"Hello?" he said as he put the phone to his ear.

"What up, blood? It's Bo."

"Man, where the fuck you been, nigga? I been trying to call you since yesterday," Mack replied, his mood improving now that he was back in contact with one of the top members of his crew.

"You not gone believe this shit. I'm in jail, dawg."

"What?" Mack yelled.

"Yeah, the pigs ran up in the mansion and took down the whole crew. We all up in here except Bad News and Baby Monster they in Juvenile Detention, you know they still minors and shit."

"How the fuck they pop y'all?" Mack couldn't believe his whole out of town crew was locked down.

"Man, that nigga Baby Monster sold a pound to some hatin' ass nigga name Happy Jack from the projects. The nigga Jack was working for the cops the whole time, so they follow Baby Monster to the spot and hit the shit the next day. But we was sitting on empty, so they trying to hold us all on one pound plus seventy-five thousand dollars," Bo explained.

"You calling three-way, nigga?"

Mack had just realized that Bo called straight through. He hoped the nigga knew better than to call his phone from a three-way.

"Naw, blood. I just bought this cell phone from one of the guards today. This shit hit me for a G."

"Ok, well shit. Just hold on tight and I'ma have all you niggas out on bond in no time."

"Ok, blood. Good looking. You can call me at this number and if I don't answer, leave a message and I'll call you right back," Bo replied before hanging up.

Mack really needed to get in contact with Rob now. He knew whatever trouble Bo and them had gotten into, Rob could easily get them out of.

"Shit, what else could go wrong?" he thought to himself.

Then he noticed the unmarked cop car that had been following him ever since he left the shop. As soon as they crossed over Prairie, the cops flashed their lights and blared the sirens, signaling Mack to pull over.

"Fuck!" he yelled as he pulled over in front of Sizzlers.

He thought about the last time he and Kat ate there. The dishwasher must have been broken, because the dishes had food stuck to them and they vowed they would never eat there again. He looked in the mirror and saw a tall white cop in plain clothing approaching the driver's side door. Reluctantly, he rolled down the window. He already had his license, registration and insurance card ready.

"Can I help you, officer?" he asked.

The officer stared down at him through mirrored sunglasses.

"You can't help me, but I might be able to help you," he replied.

Before T-Mack could figure out what he meant by the comment he just made, the cop tossed a cheap, 7-Eleven ten-dollar cell phone in his lap and walked away without saying another word. T-Mack stared at the phone as if it were a snake in his lap. When it started to vibrate, he almost jumped out the window.

"Damn, I got to stop smoking so much," he told himself.

He picked the phone up and put it to his ear.

"Hello?" he answered, not knowing who or what to expect.

"Hello to you, Travon."

As soon as the man said his name, he knew exactly who it was.

"Rob, I been trying to reach you," Mack explained.

"I need your help. Bo got himself popped along with the rest of his crew on some bullshit charges. Can you send some attorney to Atlanta to clean things up?" Mack pleaded.

"I'm afraid they're gonna have to wait. We have bigger problems to take care of."

Mack couldn't think of anything bigger than getting his crew out of jail. They were making five hundred thousand dollars a month in Atlanta and every day they spent behind bars, he was losing close to twenty thousand dollars. So he was afraid to ask what could be worse then that.

"What's the problem?" Mack probed, not really wanting to hear the answer.

"It seems your stupid cousin Michael has got himself in some serious trouble and has decided to snitch on us to get himself out."

Mack was shocked and did not know how to respond. All he could think of was all the information his cousin knew and his first thought was to flee the country. He could tell by the anger in Rob's voice that the shit was about to hit the fan.

"Who told you this? Are you sure?"

Mack knew it was true, but he had to ask, even though he knew Rob would never call him without all the facts straight first.

"Don't question me, Travon," Rob yelled through the phone.

It was Mack's first time hearing the otherwise cool Rob lose his temper.

"We are scheduled to come across the desk of a judge that owes the family a very big favor. There is a special task force trying to take us down, but what those clowns don't know is how deep this shit goes. It's way bigger than me. They want permission to tap all my phones, yours and everyone else's you can think of, so they can confirm Michael's statements. There are over twenty names on the list and this is just the beginning," he explained before going on.

"The judge is holding off on signing the warrant for 72 hours. Travon, the only way he will be able to deny the permission is if your cousin Michael comes up missing."

Mack was still parked on the side of the road in a daze. He couldn't believe what he was hearing and couldn't think of a word to say. He just sat quietly and listened.

"The only problem is we don't know where they are keeping the son of a bitch, so I don't know how you're gonna do it. But you better hope you find him before that warrant goes out. Because if you don't, I have a crew of LAPD officers – one of whom you just met -- who have strict orders to make sure you won't be around to rat me out. I hope you understand it's business, nothing personal. I just can't leave my faith in another man's hands," Rob explained.

"If you get lucky and find him and exterminate the problem, then everything will go back to normal. But for now, this will be the last time you hear from me, so you can just toss the phone out the window. We're done. Good luck," he said right before the line went dead.

Mack was still trying to grasp the scoop of what Rob had just told him as he pulled up at the front gate of his condo.

"How are you, Mr. Mack?" the gate guard asked while he opened the gate.

Mack didn't respond. He had not even noticed him standing there waving at him as he drove through the gate. He pulled around to his condo and noticed a big U-Haul blocking several car spaces and the entrance to the underground parking. He was about to honk at the driver, when Blazz jumped out and started walking towards him. He was just finishing up a conversation he was having on the phone.

"Yeah, nigga. You can get a thousand for twenty-five hundred…"

"Ok, well, just slide by Leelee spot and he will hook it up, because I'm busy right now…. Ok, later," he said, hanging up the phone.

When he saw the look on Mack's face, he knew something was wrong.

"What up, bro. You look like shit, dawg."

Mack was still trying to get a grasp on things.

"Man, you not gonna believe this shit, blood," he replied as he got out the car, leaving it parked right behind the U-Haul truck.

They headed up the stairs as he explained everything on the way.

"Man, I can't believe Solo went out like that," Blazz shook his head.

Mack went directly to the kitchen, took a bottle of Hennessey out and began to drink straight from the bottle.

"Man, how in the fuck does Rob think we supposed to find him, anyway? He's the one with all the connects," Blazz said.

He took the bottle from Mack and took a drink. Mack was in deep thought. He was trying to figure out what he should do. He loved his cousin Solo, but he had broken the laws of the street and sold the crew out to save his own ass. Mack was left with no choice but to follow Rob's orders, not to mention what would happen to him if he failed. Those crooked cops Rob had standing by would pull out all stops to track him down, take his life and kill whoever else was around, so running was really not a good option. But how in the hell was he supposed to find Solo in seventy-two hours? He couldn't find him before he went into witness protection, so what made Rob think he can find him now?

Mack raised the bottle of Hennessey to his mouth and let the alcohol burn its way down to the pit of his stomach while he contemplated his next move. He was trying to drink his troubles away, but the more he drank, the angrier he got. He wanted to kill his cousin so bad. The nigga was destroying everything Mack had worked so hard to build by running his mouth to the cops. And now he was somewhere hiding like a scared bitch. Mack wished there was some way to find him.

Then a crazy idea popped up into his head. It was so crazy it just might work, he thought.

"I think I know how to find him," he announced.

He picked up his phone and dialed Slick.

"How the fuck we gonna find him?" Blazz asked, not believing it was possible at such short notice.

He was willing to try anything to save his brother's life, however.

"We gonna make his bitch ass look for us," Mack replied with a crazy look in his eyes.

Blazz thought his brother had lost his mind or had too much to drink. How in the fuck could they make Solo come out of hiding and look for them?

⚔

"What up Mack?" Slick said.

He was sitting in his Camaro parked on the block. He sounded like he was in a good mood. He had no idea about the situation they were in.

"Check it out, blood. I got a job for you," Mack said.

He began to explain the situation to him.

When Kat arrived home, she saw Blazz and Mack loading boxes into the truck. She knew what the boxes contained and when she saw the urgent expressions on both men's faces, she could tell something was terribly wrong. She ran up to Mack. He was setting a box down in the truck.

"Is everything ok, babe?" she asked.

She could tell he had been drinking. His body reeked of sweat and alcohol.

"Look, ma. There's a lot of shit going on right now. I will fill you in later. Right now, I need you to help us load the rest of these boxes up so we can hurry up and move this truck," he explained as he turned around and headed for the elevator.

Kat followed right behind him, ready to do whatever it took to help her man. She did not even change out of her nice clothes. She just grabbed a box and headed back out. By the time they were done, Mack had told Kat everything. They were all exhausted and in bad need of showers, but first they needed to find a place to hide the truck.

"I'm take it to my parents' house and have my dad put it in the back yard," Kat announced, trying to help the situation any way she could.

Mack took her suggestion into consideration and was beginning to like the idea. He knew where Kat's parents lived and felt his money would be safe there.

"I think that's a great idea, babe," he said.

He then went over and gave her a kiss on the forehead. He loved the fact that she was not freaking out and was helping out with everything. Most women wouldn't know how to handle the fact that their man was going to have a hit out on him in less than three days if he didn't pull off a miracle. He couldn't help but notice how beautiful she was, even with her clothes all dirty and her hair pulled back into a simple ponytail. She still lit up the room. He just prayed they had more than a few days left to be together.

"Ok. I'll leave now," she replied, kissing him on the lips.

Mack was about to head for the shower, but stopped once he heard the water already running. He realized Blazz had beat him to it, so he sat down at the dining room table and had one more drink while he waited his turn.

CHAPTER 27

Slick pulled into the driveway of a small brown house on 91st. He noticed a few kids playing up the street, but other than that, it was quiet. He tightened his gloves up and pulled the hood of his sweatshirt over his head before he exited the stolen Mustang. When he reached the gate, he tried the handle, but it was locked shut. There was a black Challenger sitting on the other side of the fence, it was covered in dust. It appeared as if it had not been driven for weeks.

Slick quickly jumped the fence and rang the doorbell. A few seconds later, he saw a light come on inside. Then the wooden door swung open and a woman in her seventies peeked through the bar door that separated her from him.

"Yes, can I help you?" she asked.

Slick studied her through the bars before replying.

"Yes. Ms. Thomas, right" he asked to be sure.

The old lady was startled a bit when she heard her name from this young boy she had never seen before.

"Yes, I'm Ms. Thomas…"

Before she could complete her sentence, Slick raised his chrome fifty caliber and fired a round into her face. *Boom.* The bullet ripped through the door and hit her in the head, slamming her to the ground and nearly taking her whole head off. He peeked through the big hole in the bar door to see the damage. He saw that his job was done.

He hopped back across the fence and drove away as the neighbors started to come investigate the loud explosion.

Chapter 28

Solo sat on the second floor balcony of a federally seized Santa Monica beach house drinking coffee and watching the sunrise over the Pacific Ocean. Any minute now, a beautiful woman would be jogging by in her short shorts and spandex and still might even be in her bathing suit with sweat running down her toned body. He could hardly contain himself. He had been at the beach house ever since he was released from the hospital shortly after he agreed to cooperate with the cops. He didn't feel too bad about his decision. The only regret he had was that he would have to leave Los Angeles after the case was over. But there were other cities with nice beaches. Maybe he would relocate to Miami. He had never been there, but from what he heard their beaches were ten times better then LA's.

His cell phone rang, snapping him out of his daydream. He cheeked the caller ID and saw the call was coming from his grandmother's house, so it was either her or his crack head mother begging for a handout.

"Hello," he answered, hoping it was not his mother. Most likely it wasn't. She only showed up at the house once or twice a month when she was tired of running up and down Figueroa.

"Hello, is this Michael?" a strange voice asked.

Instantly Solo became alert, why was there a strange man calling from his grandmother's house?

"Yeah. Who the fuck is this and why you in my house?" he yelled as he stood up.

He wanted an explanation and he wanted it right now.

"Calm down, son. This is detective Rodriguez and I'm calling because your name and number was written down on a piece of paper by the side of the phone."

Solo relaxed a bit when he heard the man say he was a detective. It probably had something to do with the case he was helping with. "Oh sorry, detective. I just been a little jumpy lately. But why are you over there? I don't live there anymore."

Solo still had his guard up. He knew Rob had police on his payroll, so he was not about to reveal too much information.

"Is Margret Thomas related to you, sir?"

Solo didn't understand what that had to do with anything, but went on and answered the question anyway.

"Yes, why you ask?" he replied.

Now something deep down inside him was telling him something was terribly wrong.

"Can you please get over here?"

"What the fuck is the problem, man? If you got something to say, just spit it out!" he blurted, cutting the cop off.

He was tired of all the questions. If there was a problem, he wanted to know now. He was not about to wait any longer.

"I'm sorry to tell you, son, but she's dead. Someone murdered her last night. She was shot in the face at point-blank range. We're about to take the body to the morgue and we need to identify her as soon as possible."

Solo couldn't believe what he had just heard. He dropped the phone down, fell to his knees and cried like a baby. He couldn't believe the woman who raised him like a son because his own mother was too strung out on drugs, was gone.

He knew without a doubt who was responsible for the vicious act.

"Mack," he mumbled between sobs.

Then he pulled himself together and headed downstairs. There were two officers assigned to keep Solo safe and make sure he stayed put. One was asleep in a back room and the other was watching the six o'clock morning news when Solo entered the room. The one cop watching TV briefly looked up and nodded then went back to watching TV. Solo walked towards the man and before he knew what was happening, he had been knocked unconscious with a swift right hand to the jaw.

Solo quickly checked his pockets and found the keys to the gray un-marked Caprice that was parked outside. He grabbed the Glock forty from the cop holster and made a hasty exit out the front door.

⚑

Mack had been up all night. He hadn't gotten one wink of sleep. He was too busy making sure he had taken all the right precautions for his encounter with Solo. He and his cousin had grown up together and he knew Solo could turn into a real monster when provoked. He had definitely done that when he gave the order to have his grandmother killed. Even though she was not T-Mack's grandmother, he still felt bad about having her murdered. He re-membered when he was a kid, his father would take him and Blazz to Solo's house to play and spend the night during the weekend and summer vacation. Ms. Thomas would always make sure they stayed in the back yard when they played and would leave big pitchers of Kool-Aid on the back porch for them to drink when it was hot outside.

The alarm clock on the nightstand went off and interrupted his thoughts. It was seven-thirty, time for Kat to get up and get ready for school. He hit the off button but not before it had woke Kat. She turned over on to her back and yawned while she straightened both arms out wide. Her long black hair was all over the place. Mack brushed it out of her face with his hands and gave her a kiss on the lips.

"You like this morning breath?" she teased, and then kissed him once more before she got up and went to the bathroom.

She had one of T-Mack's t-shirts on with nothing on underneath.

"What time you have to be at school?" he called out.

He got out of bed and pulled the forty-five Hk handgun from under the pillow and put it in the waistband of the jeans he still had on from last night.

"At nine, babe," she yelled from the bathroom.

T-Mack knew that Solo would be through sometime today and he didn't want Kat around when he got there.

"Well, when you get out call me before you come home. It might not be safe for you over here until I find Solo," he explained before going in the living room to wake Blazz up.

But Blazz was already wide-awake, watching early morning cartoons and eating a bowl of Captain Crunch cereal.

"What up, bro?" Blazz said when he saw Mack walk through the door.

The TEC-9 he carried was resting on the coffee table next to the box of cereal.

"Shit, I'm just ready to get the shit over with," Mack replied.

He still had not told Blazz what he did to get Solo out of hiding and he did not plan on telling him at all. He knew how much his little brother used to like going over there to play when they were young. Blazz was fond of the old lady and Mack didn't know if he would understand the drastic measures he had to take to save all of them.

"Yeah, me too, man. I'm trying to fuck this bitch I meet the other day at the mall," he replied.

"Man you should have seen her face when she saw a young nigga pull up in a Range Rover. Bitch talking like, 'Is that your parents' car?' I was like, 'Bitch, I'm grown!'" Blazz added, then busted up laughing.

Blazz wasn't worried about the Solo situation. Mack sat down and turned to the news to see what was going on in the world.

"Man, I was watching cartoons, dawg."

"Boy, fuck cartoons. Blood, that shit is for kids. I thought you told that bitch at the mall you was grown," Mack answered.

"Don't even front like you don't watch cartoons, dawg," Blazz replied.

Kat walked in the room carrying her Louie Vuitton book bag. She had on skintight Blue jeans, black UGG boots and a black Abercrombie sweater. Her long black hair was pulled back into a Chinese-style bun complete with chopsticks and pins holding it together.

"You want something to eat, babe?" she asked Mack as she sat her bag down on the floor and walked in the kitchen.

"Naw, ma. I'm good. I ate something while you was sleep," he replied.

"Babe, we out of eggs and orange juice. Can you run to the 7-Eleven on the corner and get some please?" she called out from the kitchen.

She had already begun frying sausage and potatoes and the aroma was filling the house.

"Shit, I'll go as long as you make me some too," Blazz blurted.

He jumped up and began putting on his hoodie.

"You know I got you, Blazz," Kat replied from the kitchen.

"Damn you, greedy nigga. You just ate damn near half a box of cereal!" Mack said.

He picked the TEC-9 up off the coffee table and handed it to his little brother.

"Make sure you stay on point bro," he added.

"Man, that nigga is way too big to be sneaking up on somebody. Ray Charles could see him coming from a mile away," Blazz replied, laughing at his own joke as he headed for the door.

At the same time, Mack's cell phone began to ring. He picked it up and answered it.

"Hello?"

"The nigga here and he is on his way up."

It was Slick. He had been downstairs all night waiting for Solo to arrive.

"What?" Mack shouted.

He looked up at Blazz as he opened the door.

"Close the door, dawg!" he yelled.

He dropped the phone down and pulled his gun out, but it was too late. Standing in front of Blazz towering over him like the giant that he was, was Solo. Before Blazz could even think his young mind was erased by the forty-caliber bullet that penetrated his skull, and ripped the back of his head off. His lifeless body hit the floor and blood poured out like a spilled bottle of Champaign on the snow-white carpet.

Kat stepped out the kitchen when she heard the gun go off. She was praying that Mack was okay. She stumbled over Blazz's body but was swiftly caught by Solo's cast-covered arm. He pulled her close to him, aiming his gun at the side of her face.

"Mack, you killed my grandma, nigga," Solo shrieked.

The monster had been awakened and had now come for revenge.

"Mack, how could you, blood?"

Solo was crying. His eyes were red and his mind lost. The only thing he wanted was to make Mack pay for the pain he had caused.

"Nigga, you just killed my baby brother, your own cousin," Mack replied, his face covered in tears.

He couldn't believe Blazz was gone.

"You went out like a bitch snitching on the whole crew and I knew you was the one telling Rob all my business, nigga. You just an all around traitor," Mack blustered.

He was aiming his gun at Solo, but the love of his life was standing in the way.

"Fuck you, blood. You killed my grandma and now I'm gonna kill you and this bitch."

Kat was in shock. She hadn't heard one word that had been spoken since she'd seen Blazz's body on the floor. With the gun to her face, she was frozen, her body numb. Her eyes were wide open, but her mind was years away remembering a time in her life when she had no one to protect her from an evil and cruel world.

"You don't have to do this shit, man. Just let her go. She don't have nothing to do with this," Mack begged, lowering his gun to his side.

"Just take me. I'm the one you want."

Solo looked at T-Mack and began to laugh. He sounded like a madman.

"Ha ha ha ha. Just take you. She ain't got nothing to do with it. What the fuck my grandmother had to do with it, bitch ass nigga? You killed my fucking grandmother, blood!"

Solo slowly began to pull the trigger.

BAM! The sound of the gun going off was so loud, you could feel the vibration through the floor.

Mack had closed his eyes. Everyone he loved was now dead, he thought.

"Naw, nigga. *I* killed your Grandmother," Slick voice said as he walked through the front door and grabbed Kat checking to see if she was alright.

Mack opened up his eyes and saw that Kat was still alive while Solo lay on the floor dead next to his little brother with a bullet lodged in the back of his large head. He ran over to where Blazz lay on the floor and dropped down to his knees. He began to weep like a baby.

"No, no, no, no. It ain't supposed to end like this…"

Chapter 29

Two years later, Mack was sitting on the living room floor of his Newport Beach mansion playing with his three-month-old son while his wife Kat was outside relaxing in their hot tub. He was devastated at the loss of his brother, and if it wasn't for Kat's pregnancy, he might not have ever gotten over his loss. He still thought about his little brother every day, and he even named his son Brian after his one and only sibling.

He still had not heard from Rob, but had seen his picture on CNN several times. He was now a senator representing the State of California in the US Senate. Mack figured Rob might have decided to let him do his own thing without him, now that he had stepped up in the world. He probably had no use for a young street thug like him. The crew was still doing their thing, not only in Los Angeles and Atlanta, but they had also expanded to Florida and New York and Mack ran the whole operation without the help of Rob. But he still sent Geno to Atlanta to get Bo, Bad News, Take Off, Punch and Baby Monster out of the jam they were in once Solo was dead.

The doorbell rang, letting Mack know someone was outside. It had to be a neighbor or the mailman because they lived in a gated community by the beach, and if you didn't live there, you needed permission from one of the residents to get by the guards at the front gate. He scooped little Brian up in his arms and headed for the door.

"Who you think is at the door, little man?" he asked his son in a loving voice.

"You don't know, you just want this, huh?" he said as he held up the infant's bottle.

The baby reached for the bottle with both hands and began to suck on the nipple when Mack put it in his mouth.

"Damn son, you acting like you didn't just finish a bottle," Mack said looking at his baby boy.

He reached for the door and opened it up without checking the peephole and when he looked up, he saw a familiar face smiling at him.

"How did you get past the guards at the front gate?" Mack asked, surprised to see the man standing at his front door.

"Is that any way to greet your old friend?" replied the senator.

The end

www.ingramcontent.com/pod-product-compliance
Lightning Source LLC
Chambersburg PA
CBHW071253130626
46556CB00003B/1289